"The suspense starts on the first page and doesn't let up. A unique setting with unforgettable characters."
—Terrence McCauley, author of *Sympathy for the Devil*

"Briskly paced and precise as a Sunday crossword, this mystery hooks you fast, reels you in, and keeps you dangling in suspense till the very last page."
—Scott Adlerberg, author of *Jungle Horses* and *Graveyard Love*

"*S*tands as a glorious bastard child of *Goodfellas* and *The Golden Girls*...further cements S.W. Lauden as one of the best new voices in mystery and crime."
—Angel Luis Colón, author of *The Fury of Blacky Jaguar*

"A taut, suspenseful romp through the Redneck Riviera with an entertaining cast of characters"
—Michael Lister, author of *Innocent Blood*

"Femme fatale, Florida heat, and clues tougher to figure out than a *NY Times* Sunday crossword puzzle. *S*un-splashed noir with New York City attitude. A fun read that will keep you guessing until the end."
—Matt Coyle, author of the Anthony Award winning Rick Cahill crime series

"S.W. Lauden marches into Carl Hiassen's Florida to mark his territory with whip-crack dialogue, tight plotting, and hellfire pacing all of which will leave you gasping for breath."
—Eryk Pruitt, author of *Dirtbags* and *Hashtag*

CROSSWISE

S. W. LAUDEN

CROSSWISE

Down & Out Books
3959 Van Dyke Rd, Ste. 265
Lutz, FL 33558
www.DownAndOutBooks.com

The characters and events in this book are fictitious. Any similarity to real persons, living or dead, is coincidental and not intended by the author.

Cover design by J.T. Lindroos

ISBN: 1-943402-20-5
ISBN-13: 978-1-943402-20-5

Dedicated to Magnetic Attraction.

QUEENS

Tommy Ruzzo had unlimited access to the evidence locker at the precinct. They never could prove that he took the blow, but his law enforcement career was over either way.

Shayna Billups had bleached blonde hair, long legs and a taste for cocaine. He accepted his fate and followed her all the way to Seatown, Florida. Ruzzo traded his NYPD badge for a golf cart and polo shirt.

He had never been to the Gulf before and was mesmerized by the white sand beaches and crystal clear water. The sweaty, tropical sex was good too.

The spell broke when the drug money ran out. He soon discovered the only job he could get was as a security guard at Precious Acres Retirement Community. She left him shortly after he collected his first meager paycheck. An ex-husband named Randy Liddell emerged from the swamps and carried her off.

That was three months ago. Ruzzo got promoted to Head of Security earlier this week, two days after his thirty-second birthday.

He was currently standing over a dead body on

the bocce ball court outside the Precious Acres community center. Yesterday's edition of the *Seatown Sentinel* was placed squarely on the victim's chest. It was open to the crossword puzzle, but only the answer to one across was filled in: QUEENS.

Jesse Lee Cavanaugh, the groundskeeper who made the discovery, was leaning on a rake next to Ruzzo. In his early sixties, Cavanaugh was tall and thin with a pronounced beer belly that made him look like a recently fed snake. The bridge of his nose had been flattened a long time ago, giving him a prizefighter's profile.

"Happens all the time. They move down here from New York and just drop dead. I say good riddance."

Ruzzo's body tensed. He was five-foot-eight but stocky, with a nervous energy that made him look like a loaded spring. A late bloomer, he spent his childhood on the streets of Queens fighting off nicknames like "Little Man" and "Tiny Tommy."

He finally sprouted a few crucial inches in his late teens, but never got anywhere near his dream height of six feet. Shayna liked to call him "Little Bear" because he had a hairy chest and snored when he slept. She was the only one who ever got away with using the word "little" when describing him.

The groundskeeper was looking down on him at

the moment, trying to backtrack in a grumbly drawl.

"No offense, of course."

Ruzzo lifted his hand and wiped the sweat from his neck. Strands of his thick, black hair were plastered to his forehead thanks to the unforgiving humidity. He saw the lightning flash and dance from the corner of his eye, and waited a few seconds for the rumbling, summer thunder.

"Not many of them drop dead because their throats were slashed."

Cavanaugh pushed his straw hat back and squinted to take a closer look.

"I'll be damned. You're right."

Somebody had gone to a lot of trouble to pull the tongue down the victim's throat and out through the gaping wound. Ruzzo found the effect equally gruesome and clownish.

"I haven't seen anything that bat shit crazy since I was on the force. What do you know about Mr. Geratti?"

He motioned to the body at their feet. Cavanaugh spit at the ground.

"He was cantankerous, like all the rest of them. Terrible sense of humor."

"Nice. Happen to know what he did for a living before he retired down here?"

"No, but if I had to guess I'd say he was probably in the mob, or worked on Wall Street.

Something like that. Wait a minute, maybe he ran a deli?"

"You might want to update your clichés. A lot has happened in New York since the sixties."

"You guys don't have delis up there anymore? I'll be damned."

Ruzzo shot him a look. Cavanaugh was his neighbor, and they frequented the same bar downtown. In other words, he was the closest thing that Ruzzo had to a friend. It was another testament to the fact that Ruzzo hadn't been very social since Shayna left. Most nights he was satisfied with an old movie and a new bottle. Last night was no exception.

It must be something about the weather here in Florida. I never drank this much in New York.

"So I take it you don't know much about the victim?"

"Nope. Ain't that your job?"

"Yes and no. I'm still pretty new, whereas you've worked here since the Reagan administration. Why not dazzle me with your knowledge of the residents?"

"Well, let me see. He mostly kept to himself, except for when they were out here playing bocce ball."

"Who's 'they?'"

"Mr. Fava mostly, but Mr. Adamoli and Mr. Toma joined in now and again. They'd be out here

4

for hours, smoking cigars and gabbing."

"'Gabbing' about what?"

"Beats me. Whatever it is you old Italian guys gab about."

"Easy now, I'm less than half their age. And yours too."

"That so?"

Ruzzo caught Cavanaugh sizing him up with a raised eyebrow.

"Very funny. Sounds to me like this crew has known each other since before Florida."

"Could be."

"Good. We can start our investigation there."

"Sure enough. Did you see the tire tracks?"

Ruzzo looked over to where Cavanaugh was pointing. A small patch of mud nearby was crisscrossed with deep, knobby grooves. A sure sign that some of the local juvenile delinquents had been here. They liked to pass through after school and on the weekends, to harass the residents and occasionally rob them. Ruzzo felt like an exterminator chasing those filthy vermin around Precious Acres.

"Those little bastards wouldn't have the balls to do something like this."

"If you say so, Bubba."

Two Seatown police cruisers pulled up without fanfare. Four officers climbed out of the cars and ambled over to where Ruzzo and Cavanaugh stood.

Three of them fell in line behind a tall man with a neatly trimmed mustache, mirrored sunglasses and a trooper hat. The name "Sgt. Badeaux" was stitched to his starched uniform.

Ruzzo had seen him around town a few times, but always tried to steer clear. He never wanted to look another cop in the face and explain how he ended up a security guard in Florida. He wasn't exactly sure himself. Sgt. Badeaux walked straight up to the groundskeeper.

"Hey, Jesse Lee. What seems to be the problem?"

Ruzzo and Cavanaugh pointed to the corpse in unison. Sgt. Badeaux took a long look and started sniggering.

"If that don't beat all."

The other officers stepped around him and each took a look before quickly averting their eyes.

"Suppose we'll have to call in the medical examiner."

One of the officers scurried off. The other two stood at attention, clearly awaiting orders. Sgt. Badeaux bent down and grabbed the newspaper.

"Sentinel."

He looked up at Ruzzo and Cavanaugh, as if for affirmation. The screaming headline at the top of the page was about the new steeple on one of the local churches. Ruzzo recoiled at the way the officer was mishandling the evidence. He tried to bite his tongue, but couldn't stop from speaking up.

"I think we should—"

Sgt. Badeaux immediately rose to his full height and stepped straight into Ruzzo's face. Ruzzo could smell the dipping tobacco that was packed tightly inside of the man's lower lip. Small drops of dark brown saliva flung from his mouth as he growled.

"That's funny. I don't remember asking your opinion."

Ruzzo stiffened his neck and tried to resist the impulse to break the sergeant's nose with his forehead. That's how he'd ended many similar confrontations during his four years on the force, and found it extremely effective. But that was Queens, and the people on the receiving end were usually street thugs and lowlifes. He knew what assaulting an officer would get him here. Jail time was the least of his worries.

The truth was that Ruzzo wasn't even sure he had it in him. He could feel himself getting a little softer with every day he spent in Florida. The encroaching mellowness was starting to make him stir crazy.

"It's your investigation..."

"Damn right."

"...but I'd say this looks like a good old fashioned mob hit."

"You from New York?"

"How'd you guess?"

"You all look the same."

"Pot, kettle, black much?"

"Now you listen to me. You're in Florida, and down here we don't blame all of our problems on organized crime."

Two officers stepped forward to escort Ruzzo outside of the yellow police tape that snapped in the gusting wind. Ruzzo shook himself free and headed straight for the golf cart. He stomped on the gas pedal and tried to speed away. The most he could manage was a small jerk that sent the sunglasses toppling from his own head. Cavanaugh picked them up and chased after him on foot. Ruzzo turned a corner and disappeared behind a row of topiary flamingos.

Ruzzo was deep in thought as he wound through the endless condominium blocks of Precious Acres. He hadn't really considered returning to law enforcement, mostly because it never seemed like an option. But he guessed that whoever did this had some serious ties to New York. Maybe if he solved this murder he could return to the NYPD with his head held high. Shayna might even come around again once he was back in the uniform that caught her eye in the first place.

Or was it that evidence locker key that got her attention?

It was hard to say. What started out as a one-night stand turned into a long weekend. By Monday morning she was so strung out that a snort of cocaine was the only way to keep the party going. Shayna was officially his live-in girlfriend at the end of that first week. That's when things really started getting out of control.

He had already taken more than an ounce by the time the next Saturday rolled around. Just a pinch here and there, week by week, and they were a kilo deep within three months. A lot of it went right up her nose, which paid dividends in the bedroom. She started selling the rest of it behind Ruzzo's back at their favorite local bar. That's when internal affairs came knocking.

Ruzzo was still kicking himself for being so stupid when he spotted two of Mr. Geratti's friends playing chess in the park. A few of the local teens were just climbing onto their bikes and pedaling away from the gazebo where Mr. Fava and Mr. Toma sat. Ruzzo cranked the wheel to the left and bounced along over the grass. Neither of them looked up as he killed the engine and walked their way.

"Afternoon."

The two older men grumbled, keeping their gaze on the board between them. Mr. Fava was short and round, with spidery red veins that spread across his cheeks. There was a heavy cane between his knees that he bounced lazily from side to side.

Mr. Toma was impossibly thin and sported a bushy gray mustache that seemed to originate from somewhere deep inside of his Roman nose. Both men wore loud tropical print shirts and straw pork pie hats.

Conversations in the South were always much slower than in New York, but the senior citizens at Precious Acres were the worst. Ruzzo tried to wait patiently while Mr. Toma considered his next move. A trembling hand finally rose up and brought the knight out into the middle of the board. Ruzzo noticed that a couple of Toma's fingers were recently bandaged.

"Were those kids bothering you?"

He was fishing, but they weren't biting. Ruzzo would have to press the issue if he wanted any information before Sgt. Badeaux got to them.

"Have either of you seen Mr. Geratti today?"

Was it his imagination or did they share a brief glance? If so, it was over before Ruzzo could follow up on it. Mr. Toma turned to address him.

"You check the bocce ball courts?"

"I actually just came from there."

Mr. Fava's cane was suddenly bouncing at a faster clip. He brought a hand up to move his rook, but knocked the bishop over in his haste. Now both men turned to look at Ruzzo. He studied their rheumy, yellow eyes, looking for something to go on. They seemed to be waiting for him to leave.

"Did either of you know Mr. Geratti back in New York?"

Mr. Toma addressed his silent friend instead of Ruzzo.

"You believe this? He thinks we all lived in Little Italy together or something."

"Take it easy. I was just wondering if we might know some of the same people."

"You want to know more about us? Go ask your mother. She knew us *intimately*."

Mr. Toma banged his cane on the ground, his laughter somewhere between a cough and a gasp. It was like listening to a circus seal begging for fish.

"Hey! That's uncalled for. I was just making small talk."

"Take it somewhere else before we complain to the board and get your tin badge taken away."

Checkmate. Ruzzo stood his ground for a few more seconds, but there was really nothing left to say.

"Fine. I'll let you two get back to your game. Enjoy the afternoon."

Both men nodded, shooting daggers as Ruzzo walked away. Light drops of rain started to fall as he reached the golf cart. The sky opened up in torrents when he pulled away a few seconds later. Thunder rumbled overhead and the lightning cracked and hissed.

Mr. Adamoli was sitting under the awning outside of the security hut doing a crossword puzzle when Ruzzo pulled up.

"I just heard the bad news about Mr. Geratti. We were supposed to play bocce ball this afternoon. And now this."

Of the three septuagenarians, Mr. Adamoli looked and acted the youngest. He still had a full head of hair, for starters, and it was always carefully groomed into a sweeping silver pompadour. At the moment he was wearing pressed linen pants and a colorful button down shirt featuring several large macaws against a backdrop of palm fronds.

Ruzzo unlocked the door and invited Mr. Adamoli in. It was a tight squeeze to get around the desk that filled most of the room. Ruzzo had to move the only guest chair aside in order to close the door. The swamp cooler mounted in the window kicked in as soon as the two men took their seats.

The smell of cigar smoke that emanated from Mr. Adamoli was overwhelming in the confined space. This job had taught Ruzzo that sight and hearing weren't the only senses that dulled with age.

"How can I help you?"

"I was hoping you had more information about Jimmy."

Jimmy? All the employees referred to the

residents by last name only, but Jimmy Geratti rang a bell—even if Ruzzo couldn't put a finger on it.

"I'm sorry for your loss, but I'm not *officially* responsible for the murder investigation."

Ruzzo looked out the window and noticed that the rain had gone just as quickly as it arrived. Sharp rays of sunlight were poking out from behind a sky of billowy clouds. Mr. Adamoli slipped a plastic comb from his shirt pocket and carefully dragged it through his hair, patting as he went.

"Do you have anything to drink in this office?"

Ruzzo thought about the bottle of bourbon in his drawer. He decided it was best to wait until he was alone.

"Vending machine's just outside. I probably have some quarters in my desk."

"Come now. We're both adults here."

Ruzzo slid the drawer open and set the bottle down on the desk. He poured three fingers each into two red plastic cups and pushed one to his guest. Ruzzo knocked his back in a single swallow. The old man gave a toast and nod before taking a small sip.

"I bet you and I know some of the same people back in New York, Mr. Ruzzo. Quite a few of my acquaintances had relationships with men in your precinct. Mostly before your time, of course."

"No kidding."

Ruzzo leaned back in his chair and enjoyed the

familiar warmth in his chest. Mr. Adamoli swirled the bourbon in the cup and gave it a sniff, as if he was at a wine tasting.

"I envy you. A young man in the prime of his life. You have a good job and you live along one of the nicest beaches in the world."

Ruzzo thought it didn't sound half bad the way he put it.

"Well, we're both here now."

The old man pulled an embroidered handkerchief from his shirt pocket and dabbed at his own forehead.

"You wouldn't believe the things I did so that I could afford to retire here."

"Oh yeah? Feel like sharing?"

"It's nothing you didn't see in your previous line of work. Especially given the circumstances of your departure."

Ruzzo poured himself another shot and drank it down.

"You seem to know a lot about my time on the force, Mr. Adamoli."

"I stay in touch with friends. They tell me things. Keep me up on the latest news from the old neighborhood."

The cup sounded cheap and hollow when Ruzzo slammed it down on the desk.

"Out of curiosity, which side of the law are these 'friends' of yours on?"

"You already know the answer to that question. Let me ask you one instead: Do you miss it?"

"New York?"

"Police work."

"Like you said, I've got it pretty good down here."

"I couldn't agree more. It would be a shame to see you lose it all over a botched murder investigation on your own turf. I can't imagine you'll get many more second chances."

Mr. Adamoli brought his cup up and took another drink, keeping his eyes on Ruzzo over the rim. The humming and sputtering of the swamp cooler was the only noise as the old man stood up and carefully pushed the chair aside to open the door. Ruzzo followed him out.

"What is it exactly that you want from me?"

"Do your job, Mr. Ruzzo. Everything else will become clear in time."

The door swung shut with a soft click. Ruzzo noticed that Mr. Adamoli had left the crossword puzzle sitting on the desk. He spun the folded newspaper around. The answer to one across was filled in and circled: NEPHEW.

Ruzzo was replaying the conversation in his head when the office phone rang. He checked the number and saw that it was coming from the Precious Acres corporate offices in Tampa.

If those old bastards filed a complaint, so help me God I'll...

"Ruzzo here."

"What the hell is going on up there?"

It was Maggie Walker, Vice President of Residential Affairs and Public Relations. Ruzzo always thought her nasally voice sounded like the high-pitched whining you hear after a day at the shooting range. They had never met in person, but he imagined she was four feet tall and weighed three hundred and fifty pounds.

"Hello, Maggie. What are you going on about?"

"Oh, I don't know, *the murder maybe.*"

"Technically, it's still an open case."

"Did you become a legal expert before or after you got run out of the NYPD?"

"Take it easy. What do you want to know?"

"How on earth can something like this happen at one of our premiere retirement communities."

Ruzzo knew that "premiere" was a stretch. Precious Acres looked good in brochures, but it felt like a white-collar prison once you lived there. Of course, he couldn't say any of that to her unless he wanted another history lesson about the company.

"We have very high expectations when it comes to the safety of our residents. I shouldn't have to remind you that Precious Acres is a family owned and operated business."

"So you've told me."

Maggie practically lectured him on the legend behind Precious Acres every time they spoke. He already knew that it came into the world as the Kostbar Bros. Circus in the 1920s. That they were a regional outfit specializing in daredevil trapeze and high wire acts. Ruzzo assumed it was just a public relations spiel carefully crafted to fill beds.

Sometime in in the 1960s, when the three founding brothers reached retirement age, their adult children took over the family business. The first thing they did was to buy a small trailer park that could house their aging parents year around. The Precious Acres in Seatown was the sight of that trailer park, a fact that Maggie never let Ruzzo forget.

From circus and trailer park to slow motion funeral home. Big deal.

Maggie always got excited when she told the part about how the trailer park grew into the first Precious Acres in the late 1970s. That was right around the time when retirees from the Northeast began flocking to this part of Florida. The circus was on its last legs by then, mostly thanks to poor management. The second generation of Kostbar siblings sold the tents and animals to build their first condo community.

These days there were seven luxury retirement communities spread throughout the Sunshine State. Through it all, Precious Acres remained a family operation with a marketing slogan that said it all: "We'll treat your parents like they're our parents."

Ruzzo didn't know much about the Kostbar's parents, but he'd heard plenty about the current generation of owners. Rolf and Heidi Kostbar were infamous middle-aged twins renowned for their decadent lifestyle and public sexual conquests. He liked women of every shape and size, but they got younger as the night went on. She liked profess-sional athletes, preferably from the Dominican Republic. Neither of them ever married or had children, a fact that begged questions about the future of the organization.

Ruzzo had never been to the corporate offices, but rumors of the extravagant penthouse suite staffed with private chefs and round-the-clock masseuses were the stuff of legend. He secretly hoped to take advantage of those company perks himself one day. But getting Maggie Walker off the phone was a bigger priority at the moment.

"That's the thing with crime, it's unpredictable."

"Well it shouldn't be. Not when we pay you good money to keep our residents safe from axe-wielding psychos."

"Nobody said anything about an axe. Is that the kind of thing you corporate types make up with all of your free time?"

"Be careful, Ruzzo. There's plenty you don't know about this company."

"You'd be surprised at how much information we get out here in the sticks."

His response was met with such complete silence that he had to make sure the call was still connected.

"Maggie?"

"I don't appreciate your sarcasm. So, if you're through with your little tantrum, I'd like to hear more about the murder."

"It was a longtime resident named Jimmy, er, Mr. Geratti. Cavanaugh discovered him this morning."

She immediately brightened up.

"How is old Jesse Lee?"

"Good, I guess."

"You tell him I said 'hey.' He went to high school with my daddy."

Seems like everybody in Florida went to the same school.

"Should I go on?"

"Yes, and start from the beginning. I need to take really good notes. The Kostbars are expecting a full report by C.O.B. today."

The condos at Precious Acres were small and cramped, but they were like mansions compared to Ruzzo's living quarters. The addition of a small bathroom and kitchenette had transformed the former storage space into a "studio apartment." The thin walls had been an issue for the other residents when Shayna was still around, but things were much quieter these days. Too quiet for Ruzzo's New York ears.

His first couple of Internet searches for "Jimmy Geratti" didn't yield much useful information. It wasn't until he tried "Geratti mob" that he found a thread of news stories from 2003. It was before his time on the force, but he was familiar with the case.

DEAD MOBSTER ALIVE IN QUEENS?

Police have re-opened the search for suspected mafia hit man, Giancarlo "Jimmy" Geratti. A notorious member of a notorious crime family, Geratti has been presumed dead since disappearing in 1997. He is wanted in connection with six murders that occurred in Queens dating back to the 1980s.

The thread had been updated a few times in the following months, but Geratti was never found. Ruzzo's subsequent image searches only turned up a couple of blurry, declassified surveillance photos from a failed federal sting operation. But he had his answer either way—Jimmy Geratti was still at large, and probably had plenty of powerful enemies.

Ruzzo didn't know what he had stumbled into, but it was getting bigger by the second. His mind was reeling as he pushed his chair back and went over to the lone kitchen cupboard. The middle shelf was stocked with a few bottles of bourbon and little else. He filled a pint glass with ice and gave himself a generous pour. The part of his brain that thought like a cop was a little out of practice. Booze helped.

This case might be my ticket back to New York, but it's only going to get more dangerous.

It was only a few steps from the kitchen to his bed. He set the glass down on the nightstand and dropped to the carpet. The safe was against the wall under the headboard. He fished it out and spun the wheels on the lock. The familiar weight of the Smith & Wesson revolver felt good in his hand. He had his finger on the trigger and almost squeezed off a shot in response to the unexpected pounding on the door.

Ruzzo placed the gun back in the safe, hastily pushing it under his bed. He took another gulp of bourbon and went to look through the peephole. A young Seatown police officer was staring back at him.

He opened the door a crack. His guest helped him open it the rest of the way. Ruzzo was impressed that one of Sgt. Badeaux's flunkies could make his own decisions.

"We're questioning all employees in connection with the murder."

Typical small town police procedure. Start with the easy answers and hope to get lucky before you really have to roll up your sleeves. All of Ruzzo's experience was screaming that this was not an inside job.

"Do you have some new information that makes us all suspects?"

"You can discuss that with Sgt. Badeaux."

Ruzzo knew he wouldn't get anything but questions down at the station.

"What about the nephew?"

It was a long shot, but he could see from the look on the dimwitted officer's face that he'd struck a nerve.

"Just shut up and come with me."

NEPHEW

The police cruiser drove out of the Precious Acres security gates and turned left onto the highway. It was a two-lane affair with a speed limit that dropped to twenty-five miles per hour as it crawled through Seatown. The police station was right downtown on a sandy spit of beachfront property that doubled as a mall.

Many of the locals who weren't employed by Precious Acres made their entire yearly income there, selling overpriced groceries and souvenirs during the three months each year the town was overrun by tourists.

The leeches in Times Square got nothing on these polite Southern scammers.

He watched out the window as the vacationing families pedaled by on their rental bikes, oblivious to the news of the murder. It was hard to judge what kind of havoc an unsolved case like this could wreak on such a fragile ecosystem. He definitely didn't envy Sgt. Badeaux at the moment.

They arrived at the station five minutes later. The building itself wasn't anything to write home about, just some whitewashed clapboards on a square frame. But the powdery sand dunes that surrounded it, speckled with willowy sea oats and blooming beach sunflowers, made it look like something from a postcard. Ruzzo had been by the building a hundred times and still couldn't tell if was built in 1890 or last year.

Cavanaugh was leaving Sgt. Badeaux's office as the officer approached with Ruzzo. The grounds-keeper winked and flashed a yellow smile.

"Good luck in there. We should trade notes back at Precarious Acres."

"Precarious Acres" was a nickname that many locals used for Precious Acres ever since the bankruptcy filing. Ruzzo thought the clever nick-name was like almost everything else in Florida, a little too obvious.

"Sounds good."

The officer gave a light knock on the hollow wooden door before swinging it open. Sgt. Badeaux was sitting dead center against the far wall with his back to the window. His feet were up on the desk in the middle of the room. He still had the mirrored sunglasses and trooper hat on. Ruzzo wondered if he slept in them.

It was in Ruzzo's best interest to let Sgt. Badeaux speak first, but he was immediately impatient—and thirsty. He took the seat opposite and waited for almost three seconds.

"How's the investigation going?"

Sgt. Badeaux sized him up before he responded.

"The State Attorney's breathing down my neck, if you really want to know. Same with the suits at your corporate offices. Question is, how's *your* investigation going?"

Ruzzo was prepared for this.

"I've had a few casual conversations with some of the residents. Nothing out of the ordinary for the Head of Security."

Ruzzo liked the way it felt to say his new title out loud. Sgt. Badeaux wasn't nearly as impressed.

"I had a conversation with your old chief in New York."

That was a little more surprising. Ruzzo decided to show no fear.

"I haven't spoken to Sullivan in ages. How's that old S.O.B. doing?"

"Better now that you're gone. Said you had the makings of a pretty god cop, until you screwed up. Seem about right?"

"There are dirtier cops than me who are still on the job."

"He also mentioned that you're a college boy. I guess that explains why you think you're so much smarter than everybody around here."

"Did he have anything good to say about me?"

"As a matter of fact, he did. Said you have a certain knack for getting information out of people. That true?"

25

"I can be persuasive when I need to be."

"Good. I'd like to know exactly what you've found out about my case."

Ruzzo knew that Sgt. Badeaux might be playing both good cop and bad cop. He'd done it several times himself. First you offer them a cigarette, and then you put it out on their arm.

Badeaux's lip curled into a sneer, as if he could hear Ruzzo's thoughts.

"Go on, impress me."

"And if I don't want to help you?"

"We'll show you a little Southern hospitality in one of our cells until the investigation is over."

Bad cop always wins.

"Fine, but first you answer one question for me. What do you know about Geratti's nephew?"

"Color me impressed. Okay, I'll play along—but don't test me. Mr. Geratti's closest living relative is a nephew named Tony Geratti. Forty-two, lives in New York with his wife and three kids. Runs some sort of waste management company. No prior record. We're trying to get him to come collect the body in the next few days."

Ruzzo thought Tony Geratti sounded straight out of central casting for a mob flick.

He probably has a fuhgetaboutit *tattoo.*

"Seems pretty open and shut to me. You just need to find out who's trying to send a message to the nephew."

"I'm not so convinced. Nine times out of ten a murder happens in the heat of the moment, without any premeditation. But that's enough beating around the bush. Tell me what you've figured out."

Ruzzo recounted his conversations with Mr. Fava and Mr. Toma. Sgt. Badeaux stifled a laugh when he got to Mr. Adamoli's crossword puzzle theory. Ruzzo finished by sharing the research he'd done on Jimmy Geratti.

Sgt. Badeaux responded with two words when Ruzzo finally finished.

"Sounds complicated."

"It ain't perfect, but it's what I know so far."

Sgt. Badeaux's sneer was back, only with teeth this time.

"What you *know*, or what you're guessing at?"

Ruzzo was still formulating his come back when one of Sgt. Badeaux's squad swooped in to escort him out. The officer walked him back to the police cruiser, but Ruzzo declined the ride.

"Think I'll walk. I need some fresh air."

What he really needed was a stiff drink. Luckily, his favorite bar was right around the corner. Ruzzo waited for his escort to go back into the police station before he made a beeline for the nearby harbor.

There probably was a time when The Rusty Pelican was filled with Parrot Heads sipping on fruity rum drinks and rocking out to "Cheeseburger

In Paradise." Since then it had devolved into a dirty dive bar that served lukewarm beer and cheap booze to down-and-out locals in between unemployment checks. Shayna brought Ruzzo there when they first moved to town because she liked the '90s music in the jukebox. He liked it because it reminded him of the New York he grew up in.

Creed was blaring from the speakers as Ruzzo entered. There was a hand-drawn poster tacked to the wall advertising a "Comedy Open Mic Night EVERY Monday". He kept his gaze on the floor, trying not to make eye contact with the two worn out women sitting at a table near the front door. He'd gone home with both of them a few weeks back for a flabby threesome that left him bruised and battered. The two women had been on the prowl for an encore ever since.

Ruzzo climbed up onto a stool at the back corner of the bar. The bartender threw a cocktail napkin down and leaned in to take his order.

"You still recovering from your birthday?"

"Hey, Mikey. Let's do a beer and a shot of whisky."

Mikey's mullet swung like a curtain as he spun around to make Ruzzo's drinks. His body stayed perfectly still while his tattooed arms stabbed at the coolers and shelves in front of him. It was like watching a martial arts master in his dojo, only Mikey was a bloated middle-aged fisherman.

He set the can of beer down and slid the shot glass next to it. The bottle of whisky was still in his shaky hand, ready for a quick refill. Ruzzo obliged, pleased that the bartender knew him so well. He put that one down too and motioned for a third.

"Rough day?"

"You wouldn't believe me if I told you."

"Yeah, that's what I heard."

Word spread fast. Ruzzo changed the subject.

"What's with the poster out front?"

"Comedy night? It's something new we're trying. Business is pretty slow on Monday nights. We did the first one a couple weeks ago."

"Any good?"

Mikey nodded to the small stage in the corner.

"Mostly. I talked Cavanaugh into getting up there."

"No shit. What the hell gave you that bright idea?"

"You know he was a comedian back in the seventies, right? Used to go on the road and everything."

"He never mentioned it. How'd he do?"

"Truth? He kind of freaked out. It was a total train wreck."

Ruzzo chuckled.

"That's too bad. Was it stage fright or something?"

"Hell if I know. You can ask him about it yourself sometime. Other than that it's been going pretty well. Turns out there are some pretty funny people around here. You should stop by one of these Mondays."

"Yeah, right. I'm not getting up on stage to tell jokes."

"I was actually thinking you could be the bouncer."

"Go to hell."

Mikey was whistling along to a Matchbox 20 song as he went down the bar to fill some orders. Ruzzo took a drink, trying to imagine a young Jesse Lee Cavanaugh alone on the road. His father once told him that the friends you make as an adult would always remain a mystery. Ruzzo never really knew what that meant until he moved to Florida.

It wasn't long before Mikey was back.

"So what are you going to do about Shayna?"

An electric current shot down Ruzzo's spine at the mention of her name.

"What about her?"

"I heard she was back in town."

Ruzzo wasn't surprised to find the door unlocked when he arrived at his apartment. Shayna constantly forgot her keys when she lived there, which meant she had to pick the lock almost every night. It got to the point that the bolt wouldn't even engage most of the time when Ruzzo came and went. He considered putting in another fix-it request with the maintenance crew, but knew they had their hands full with the residents.

He was so drunk when he walked in that it took him a minute to notice the empty gun locker sitting wide open on top of the bed. An embroidered handkerchief was neatly folded and laying where the Smith & Wesson should have been. He took a slug from the bottle on the counter and went to pay Mr. Adamoli a visit.

Sinatra was blaring through the door when Ruzzo arrived. It felt like he was responding to a noise complaint. He knocked loudly a couple of times before finally trying the knob.

Mr. Adamoli was sitting in the darkened living room wearing a pinstriped suit. He lifted the remote and brought the volume down to a whisper.

"Please, take a seat. I assume you got the little clue I left you?"

Ruzzo squinted his eyes to scan the room.

"No disrespect, but I'm just here for my gun."

He dropped down on the couch opposite Mr. Adamoli. There was a crystal decanter full of bourbon on the coffee table in front of him, along with a bucket of ice and a single chiseled glass. Today's *Sentinel* and a ballpoint pen were right beside them. Mr. Adamoli cleared his throat to speak.

"Please, help yourself. I have some important information to share. You might as well get comfortable."

Resistance was futile. Ruzzo poured a drink and settled back to listen. Mr. Adamoli motioned to the newspaper.

"What you're looking for is right there."

"I'm listening."

"It used to be that we could conduct our business without much interference. But things got more complicated when the Feds started their witch hunts."

"They tend to frown on organized crime."

Mr. Adamoli cringed.

"We all live in glass houses, Mr. Ruzzo."

"Fair enough."

"The wire-tapping and constant surveillance almost put us out of business. So we took some of the money we used to give to our friends in law enforcement and funneled it to newspapermen instead."

"To spread misinformation?"

"Quite to the contrary. We only needed them to send precisely the right information to the right person at exactly the right time."

The bourbon was going down easier than Mr. Adamoli's tall tales. But he was a resident after all, and Ruzzo had to admit that he kind of liked him.

What's the harm in humoring the old nut job?

"One across?"

"Precisely."

"So you order a hit, but leave out who the specific target is because of the Feds? That seems a little imperfect."

"There's a bit more to it. I'm keeping things simple in the interest of time."

"But the nephew isn't the one who got whacked."

"Only one of us has a connected nephew, Mr. Ruzzo."

"And this crossword puzzle tradition is being carried on down here by you and your cronies?"

"Oh no. You misunderstand me. I am just telling you that I have seen certain patterns forming. It's up to you to decide who's responsible for what."

"Okay, let's say you're on to something. Why tell me instead of Sgt. Badeaux?"

"You disappoint me. I doubt very much that a Florida police officer could appreciate crimes of this nature. This has New York written all over it. And you've got New York coursing through your veins."

The old man rose slowly from his chair and wandered from the room. Ruzzo listened to him shuffling down the hall until he reached the bedroom. Mr. Adamoli had one more thing to say before he retired for the evening.

"Do the puzzle tomorrow morning. First clue, crosswise."

Ruzzo finished his drink and set the glass down on the coffee table. The handle of his gun was just visible under the newspaper. He stuck it in his waistband and headed for the door.

SHADES

The empty bottle rolled from Ruzzo's hand and banged against the hardwood floor. He sprang up in a daze, groping wildly in the bed for his gun.

He went over to the pantry and twisted the lid on his last bottle. The warm bourbon felt like it was tearing him apart as he crept over to the window. He pushed the mini blinds aside with the barrel of his revolver and looked out across the pre-dawn stillness. A golf cart came into view, the driver tossing newspapers onto porches as he crawled along. Ruzzo waited for the silence to return before he slipped downstairs to steal a *Sentinel* from one of his neighbors.

He was standing on the colonnaded porch in boxer shorts and a wife beater T-shirt when something whizzed by his head and exploded against the brick wall. Ruzzo ducked for cover just as a second egg caught him in the back. The gooey splatter gave him the sensation that he had been shot. He looked up in time to see three teenage boys howling as they pedaled off.

Back upstairs, Ruzzo took his clothes off and left them in a pile near the door. He was completely naked as he slid the flimsy newspaper from the plastic sheath and saw the crossword on the back page. The only other time he had done a puzzle was during an all-night stake out.

Ruzzo folded the paper until only the crossword grid and clues were visible. He read one across. "They look cool when it's hot."

He counted six empty boxes and tried to will himself to have the answer. When nothing came he moved on to one down, which only had three empty boxes. "Transgression of divine law."

He thanked his Catholic school years for the answer and filled it in: SIN. The answer to one across came much easier now that he knew the first letter was "S." He mulled it over for a second before spelling it out: SHADES.

Sgt. Badeaux could be the next victim, if the old man's telling the truth.

The thought crossed Ruzzo's mind before he could even put the pen down.

Or maybe somebody's trying to send Sgt. Badeaux a message.

He felt ridiculous even thinking it.

But that would be one hell of coincidence.

Ruzzo's head was spinning. Coffee was necessary to face the day ahead. He filled the bottom of his cup with milk and bourbon and watched the pot brew. A soft dinging sound came from his laptop to indicate that he had a new email. He flipped it open and saw the subject line "Little Bear."

> I'll be in Seatown tomorrow. I have a couple things to show you.
>
> xoxo, me

Ruzzo read the email several times to make sure he hadn't missed anything. It was just as cryptic the fifth time as the first. He closed the computer, filled his mug and took it into the bathroom for a cold shower.

He was deep in thought when he toweled off ten minutes later. It was impossible to know what might happen with Shayna tomorrow. Whatever it was, Ruzzo had to admit that he was excited about seeing her again. Even after all the chaos she caused.

The sudden flood of memories reminded him of something. He reached into the cabinet and sprayed himself with the musky cologne that Shayna had given him in New York. She always said that it reminded her of Florida, and that he was irresistible with it on. It was the first time he'd worn it since she left.

Ruzzo put his gun back into the safe before he left the apartment. It was already hot and sticky when he stepped outside. The newspaper was under his arm as he walked to his golf cart. He couldn't find his polo shirt in the rush to get out of the apartment, so he was stuck wearing the "I♥NY" T-shirt that Shayna had shoplifted for him.

He hadn't seen it in a few weeks, but it was sitting out on a chair when he woke up that morning. It wasn't unusual for him to get a little emotional after a few too many drinks, just like his father used to do. They were both sentimental clowns when it came to love. He was embarrassed at the mental image of himself stumbling around his apartment, clutching the shirt like some lovesick teenager. He assumed that's what happened during his blackout the previous night and it made him cringe.

But he liked the shirt so he put it on. It went well with his cologne.

He slid the crossword into the glove compartment and started making his way out to the police station. There was still a little time to kill, so he swung by the gazebo along the way. Mr. Fava was sitting there alone with the *Sentinel* folded in his lap.

"Where's Mr. Toma this morning?"

"No idea. He should've been here an hour ago."

Ruzzo decided to try and catch him off guard.

"What'd you get for one across?"

The old man set the pen and paper down and leaned back in his chair. Ruzzo could almost see the gears grinding inside of his bald, spotted head.

"I'm useless with the crossword. That's more Mr. Adamoli's thing, if you know what I mean."

The police sirens came out of nowhere. Both men watched as the cruisers sped by in the direction of the recreation center. Ruzzo rushed for his golf cart and chased behind. Several officers were standing in a circle, silently looking down at the grass when he arrived.

I might already be too late to save Sgt. Badeaux's life.

Ruzzo was starting to wish he had brought his gun with him. The killer could still be nearby, waiting to ambush them and kill a few more cops. He was only fifty yards away when he saw the trooper hat rise up from the center of the huddle. Sgt. Badeaux had simply been kneeling to inspect the body. Ruzzo was surprised by his own sense of relief.

He was about to walk over to join the officers when Sgt. Badeaux's mirrored sunglasses locked onto his T-shirt. Each of the remaining officers turned to face him. They all had their hands on their holsters now. The posse inched toward him, revealing Mr. Toma's corpse at their feet. A wire was wrapped tightly around his throat and a crude smile had been carved into his cheeks, upward from the corners of his mouth. Blood was still trickling from his chin and onto his "I♥NY" T-shirt.

Ruzzo slowly put his hands on his head and dropped to his knees. Sgt. Badeaux reached him first.

"Will you stop being so dramatic? Stand up."

"It kind of looked like you guys were getting ready to shoot me."

"What, because of your T-shirt? I guess we have shot people for less."

More sniggering from the peanut gallery. Ruzzo really didn't like being on this side of the law. He had never missed his badge as much as he did at that moment.

"It is quite a coincidence, you two dressed the same on the day he gets murdered."

Ruzzo hadn't noticed that Mr. Toma was wearing the same Precious Acres-issued khaki shorts he was. This was looking less and less like a coincidence with every passing moment.

"Why would somebody kill Mr. Toma and dress him up like me?"

"Good question, but one thing's for sure. You would need to have a serious screw loose to do something like that yourself."

"I'm glad you think so. I was getting pretty worried there for a minute."

Maybe it wasn't me who got this old shirt out last night.

A different image of the previous night began to form in his mind. One in which somebody picked the lock on the front door and went through his things while he was passed out cold. Sgt. Badeaux brought him back from his dark daydream with an unexpected question. It felt like a slap across the face.

"Have you seen Shayna Billups recently?"

Ruzzo's stomach dropped.

"No, but I heard she's back in town. I got an email from her this morning."

"Interesting. When's the last time you had contact with her before that?"

"A few months, maybe. Wait—you don't think she had something to do with these murders?"

"It wouldn't be the first time that girl brought trouble back to town with her. She's always been like a hurricane."

"That's ridiculous. I think you're way off base here."

"Want the chance to prove me wrong?"

"Yes, if it'll get Shayna off the suspect list."

"Good. I think you're about to come out of retirement."

REST

Sgt. Badeaux and his team definitely favored simple sting operations over the more complicated ones Ruzzo was used to. After a quick overview of the plan, they told him to respond to Shayna's previous email and ask to meet up. He did as instructed and she replied within minutes. They were supposed to have lunch later in the day and, if things went well, maybe grab a drink at The Rusty Pelican afterward.

Ruzzo couldn't resist fantasizing about where a few cocktails could lead, even though he would be wearing a wire. It made the whole fantasy a little impractical. He knew that Shayna wouldn't necessarily mind if a few of Seatown's finest listened in, he just wasn't sure if he could handle the scrutiny.

But there were bigger problems to worry about at the moment. At the top of the list was the assignment that Sgt. Badeaux had given him. During his reunion with Shayna, Ruzzo was also supposed to work in a few carefully crafted questions about her ex-husband. It seemed like Randy Liddell might be the real target of this sting operation, but Ruzzo couldn't get a straight answer out of Sgt. Badeaux when he asked about it.

"You sure I'm the right guy for the job? I've never even met her ex."

"Those two are thick as thieves. If one of them is involved, then both of them probably are."

"But—"

"Save the rest of your questions for Shayna."

Asking those questions was exactly what Ruzzo was dreading, for many reasons. First of all, it wasn't a topic that they had ever discussed before. Ruzzo never even knew of Liddell's existence prior to Shayna's sudden departure. Liddell was like a ghost and Ruzzo didn't know he was being haunted until it was too late.

Secondly, Ruzzo wasn't sure that he was emotionally prepared to hear what she had to say about the man who stole her away. Ruzzo had never even seen a picture of him. He kind of preferred it that way.

Beyond all of that there was a bigger issue that kept him tossing and turning for most of the previous night. Was the chance to get his badge back really worth risking any kind of future with Shayna? He knew that she might not see it that way, even if he was doing it to clear her name.

He was still grappling with that one as he closed his apartment door and headed downtown. There were a few hours to kill before lunch and he wanted to pay a visit to the *Sentinel* offices. Sgt. Badeaux might be more willing to consider the crossword puzzle theory once he was convinced of Shayna's innocence. Ruzzo wanted to be prepared when they reached that point, no matter how crazy it sounded. It was the best lead they had.

The *Sentinel* offices were right around the corner from the police station, just like everything else in Seatown. He pushed the door open and a little bell rang overhead. A short, white-haired man was standing behind the counter with a phone to his ear. Thick, black glasses were resting on top of his head. He brought them down to study his visitor, clearly surprised at the intrusion.

Ruzzo took a seat against the opposite wall and picked up a copy of the newspaper, stunned by the screaming headline: "SERIAL KILLER IN SEATOWN!" A candid picture of Sgt. Badeaux at yesterday's crime scene took up most of the page, along with a sensational caption: *Lock your doors and load your guns. Murderer on the loose.*

He flipped to the crossword puzzle and read the first clue. "Time for one's self."

It was a four-letter word, but nothing immediately came to mind. The man called out to him in a croaky voice.

"Can I help you?"

Ruzzo stood and approached the counter. The man took a few nervous steps back.

"I need to speak with the manager, or whatever you call the boss around here."

"I'm the receptionist, and the janitor, and the owner. But most people with any sense just call me the editor. Name's Billy Randolph."

"Nice to meet you. I'm Tom—"

"I know who you are. You're here about the murders. Am I right?"

"I guess you are."

"Come on back."

He pushed a swinging door open and Ruzzo stepped into the tiny newsroom. Just about every flat surface on this side of the counter was covered in stacks of old newsprint. Randolph led him to the back corner where a small desk overlooked the ocean through a dingy window. It was a criminal waste of a priceless view.

"Please, take a seat."

Ruzzo sat with his back to the window. Randolph dropped into a squeaky leather chair. He opened the top drawer of his desk and squinted at something inside before spinning to face a large black safe against the wall. It was the kind of thing that bank robbers would try to dynamite in an old cowboy movie.

"Is that an antique?"

"It came with the place. They don't make safes this sturdy anymore."

Randolph twisted the wheel and opened the heavy door. He fished around inside for a moment before producing a small microcassette recorder. It took Ruzzo a moment to realize what it was.

"You know they make digital recorders now."

"I sure do. And there'll be something even newer when this thing finally breaks. But until then..."

Randolph hit "Record" and set the device on the desk. Ruzzo hit the "Stop" button.

"Hold on a minute. I didn't come here to be interviewed."

"Why else would the prime suspect in a murder investigation come to see a reporter if not to clear his name?"

"What? I don't know who told you that—"

Randolph hit "Record" again and repositioned the device between them. Ruzzo finished his sentence before reaching out to hit "Stop" again.

"—I killed those people."

"Stop fiddling with my recorder."

Ruzzo slapped Randolph's hand away before he could reach the button this time.

"Knock it off. I am not the prime suspect. I'm here as a representative of the Precious Acres security team."

"Ha! That's just like Precarious Acres to send a

thug over here to silence the press. Did their little minion Maggie Walker put you up to this? You can tell her that I see right through the lies she tries to spread. I didn't fall for it the last time I interviewed her, and I'm not falling for it this time either. None of you can stop me from printing the truth."

His face was red and his chest was heaving. Ruzzo was genuinely concerned that the old man was going into cardiac arrest.

I should have paid more attention during those CPR classes the NYPD made me take.

"Calm down. Nobody from Precious Acres even knows I'm here."

"Going rogue, huh?"

Ruzzo decided to stop fighting the old man's Woodward and Bernstein act and just join in. Playing up to paranoid old men was becoming a specialty of his.

"You and I both know that something bigger is going on here. Help me solve this case and, when it's over, you'll get the exclusive."

"Why should I trust you?"

"Because I've got all the dirt on Precious Acres."

Randolph leaned back in his chair and folded his arms. The corners of his mouth were slowly curling into a wicked grin.

"Do we have a deal?"

"I suppose we do. What do you want to know?"

Ruzzo took a deep breath. All of this acting was exhausting, but probably good practice for later in the day.

"Who creates your crossword puzzles?"

"My what?"

"I'm asking the questions right now."

"Suit yourself. The *Sentinel* is a co-op. Lots of different people volunteer their time. Even a few residents from over at that corporate mausoleum where you work."

"Who exactly?"

"Oh, I can't keep all those Italian surnames straight. The one they found yesterday used to come in sometimes."

"His name was Mr. Toma."

"Right. Like I said, we have lots of volunteers. I'm proud to say that I could drop dead tomorrow and the *Sentinel* would keep right on publishing. But enough about me. Why are you so curious about the crossword puzzle?"

"I can't explain right now. It's part of something bigger than both of us. Everything will become clear in time."

Ruzzo went to stand up. Randolph didn't budge.

"That's it?"

"Thanks for your help."

It was getting close to lunchtime and Ruzzo still needed to stop by the police station for the wire. He thought he had gotten the answers he was looking for anyway, at least for now—until Randolph went on.

"Does this have something to do with the third twin?"

"The what?"

"Don't play dumb with me. Everybody knows there was a third Kostbar sibling that went missing twenty years ago."

"Wait. They were triplets?"

"Yep. Rolf, Heidi and poor old Peter. His yacht disappeared without a trace on a perfectly calm night. He was never heard from again."

"No shit. Is that common knowledge?"

"Of course, but nobody really talks about it. Especially with those ugly paternity claims that pop up from time to time. Peter was quite the playboy. Had women all over the state."

"Did any of them stick?"

"Nope. They all seem to get really quiet just as soon as they speak up."

"You think the Kostbars are paying them off?"

The bell at the front door rang. Randolph didn't even acknowledge the question as he shuffled over to the counter. Ruzzo waited around for a while to get more information about the Kostbar triplets, but Randolph had clearly moved on.

It was getting close to lunchtime. Ruzzo decided he would try to swing back by the *Sentinel* after he met with Shayna. Or first thing in the morning, depending on how the night went.

Sodee's Diner was Shayna's favorite restaurant in the whole wide world. On several occasions during their time together Ruzzo had introduced her to iconic New York dishes, but she always compared them to Sodee's. Mile-high corned beef sandwiches with Swiss cheese, sauerkraut and Russian dressing paled in comparison to a Sodee's Reuben. Lobster Newberg couldn't hold a candle to Sodee's Seafood Spaghetti. General Tso's Chicken? Sodee's didn't serve Chinese food, so Shayna doesn't like it.

Ruzzo walked across the sun-bleached parking lot and approached the train car facade. Sgt. Badeaux's instructions to "get Shayna talking about her relationship with Liddell" echoed in his mind as he stepped inside. An elderly waitress in a poodle skirt and pink blouse greeted him at the register.

"Hey you! Long time."

She led him through the restaurant, snapping gum in time to the 1950s sock hop music. Shayna's oversized sunglasses and handbag were sitting on the table at their usual booth, but she was nowhere to be seen. He took a seat and was reading the unchanged menu when he heard her voice.

"What do you think?"

Her enormous new boobs were inches from his

face when he looked up. He closed his eyes and breathed in the sweet smell of her perfume.

"Come on, you goofball. Check these things out."

"Wow. When did you get that done?"

"A few weeks ago. Pretty amazing, right?"

"They're definitely hard to miss."

"You're so sweet. Now stand up and give me a hug."

He barely got to his feet before she squealed and threw herself at him. She was even curvier than he remembered. It was killing him to keep her at a distance, but he couldn't risk her discovering the wire.

Ruzzo moved to the side and gave her a peck on the cheek instead. She took it in stride and eventually calmed down enough to slide into the booth. He sat right next to her and tried to strike a natural pose. It was show time.

"What are you wearing?"

"Sorry?"

"Your cologne. It's the one I got you, right?"

"I guess it is. It totally slipped my mind."

"Meow!"

She reached out to paw at his chest like a kitten playing with a ball of yarn. He leaned back and tried to pivot.

"So what's new? I mean besides the obvious."

"I suppose the big news is that Randy and I got remarried."

There it was, and much sooner than he expected. Any hope he had of winning her back seemed to drain right out of him. Shayna must have seen the look of despair on his face because she immediately started back pedaling.

"Let's talk about something else. I heard you got a promotion."

"That's true. 'Head of Security.'"

"Congrats, stud!"

She leaned over and gave him a wet kiss on the cheek. He was sure that her bright red lipstick left a mark, the way it did on everything her mouth touched. The waitress came over before he could turn the conversation back to Shayna and Liddell.

"Go ahead, baby. Order for us. Just like old times."

The waitress spoke up before Ruzzo could.

"Let me guess? The usual."

Some couples have a song. Ruzzo and Shayna had "two root beer floats and gravy fries." The waitress smiled and shuffled off to place their order.

"So, tell me where you've been."

"Tommy, baby. I'm so sorry I ran out on you and that I haven't been in touch. I owe you so many apologies."

"It all feels like a hundred years ago."

"I don't even know where to start. I mean, that business with the cocaine in New York and you losing your job—"

Ruzzo brought his hand up to stop her. The last thing he needed was a police recording of this discussion, especially now that he might have a way back in with the NYPD. And what good would come of rehashing it anyway? She might have helped make the bed, but he was the only one laying in it.

"That's all ancient history, Shayna."

He thought he might be playing it a little too cool, until tears started forming in her eyes. That was a good sign. She began whimpering when he reached over to wipe them away. That was even better.

Maybe I still have a shot with her after all.

"What's up, Shayna? You can tell me."

"Everything's all screwed up. I'm in way over my head...and..."

"And what? Is he hurting you?"

"Yes."

She whimpered and tried to lay her head on his shoulder. He managed to turn away. She took a couple of stuttering breaths and tried to pull herself back together.

"I don't blame you for not wanting to touch me after the way I've treated you."

"It's ancient history. You got nothing to apologize for."

She forced a smile, blinking away the last of her tears.

"Well, at least it'll make a pretty good story one day."

The waitress arrived with their food, setting it down. Shayna slid to the far side of the booth.

"Go ahead and start. I just need to freshen up."

Ruzzo was starving. He shoveled a gooey mass of fried potatoes and gravy into his mouth. A pocket of grease burst as he chewed, little blisters immediately forming on the inside of his cheek. He lunged for his root beer float. The glass crashed to the table and the sticky liquid splashed all over his clothes. He jumped up just in time to see Shayna through the window, tearing out of the parking lot in her little red convertible.

He muttered "fuck" under his breath and ran out the front door. It was possible that Shayna had seen the wire, but more likely that she had gotten overwhelmed. She'd deserted him on more than one occasion during their time together, before she finally left him for good.

His cell phone started buzzing before he reached the highway. Sgt. Badeaux was the last person he wanted to talk to at the moment, or so he thought.

"I can explain."

"I should hope so. This situation is a hot mess.

We had three prospects cancel tours today alone. At this rate we'll be out of business before the end of the week."

"Maggie?"

"You were expecting somebody else?"

"Now's really not a good time."

"I couldn't agree more. I was thinking tomorrow might be better. In person."

"Are you coming to Seatown?"

"Nope. You're coming to Tampa, to meet with the Kostbars. It's going to be a long day, so make sure you get plenty of rest tonight."

The answer to one across finally came to him as he hung up: REST.

THREE

The debriefing with Sgt. Badeaux went just like he suspected it would.

"You're a fuck up, Ruzzo. Goddamnit! I should have known better than to trust you with this."

"It was out of my control. I can make it right."

"Give me the wire."

"He's beating her. You have to stop him."

"We heard everything she said. Unfortunately, she isn't the most reliable witness."

Ruzzo watched the small brown tobacco bubbles forming at the corners of Sgt. Badeaux's mouth as he spoke. He found it almost as disgusting as this so-called small town justice.

"What the hell is that supposed to mean?"

"Get your blinders off, Ruzzo. Shayna Billups has been putting this town through hell since she got out of diapers. Nobody knows that better than Randy Liddell."

Ruzzo lifted his shirt and pulled the tape from his chest, ripping out tufts of hair in the process. One of the officers took the equipment from him before the second led him to the door. Ruzzo turned to look over his shoulder, but Sgt. Badeaux was already gone.

The memory was playing on repeat in his head as the plane landed in Tampa the next morning. Thankfully it was a short flight, the kind of business trip you could turn around in an afternoon. He probably should have been more worried about his job, but he knew it would be a hell of a lot cheaper to fire him over the phone.

The *Sentinel* crossword puzzle was sitting on the seatback tray next to his bloody Mary. The clue for one across was easy. "The magic number?" He got it instantly: THREE.

Ruzzo made his way through the sprawling Tampa airport, dodging tourists as he walked. He followed the signs to the baggage claim area, secretly hoping that a limo driver would be standing there holding up a sign that read RUZZO. It was no surprise when his little fantasy didn't come true. A taxi would have to do.

He gave the driver the address and sat back to enjoy the ride downtown. They hadn't even driven three minutes, however, when the taxi pulled up to a squat brick building situated on the edge of a long-term airport parking lot. Ruzzo assumed there was something wrong with the car.

"We're here. Airport minimum is twenty dollars."

"Are you fucking kidding me? You must have misunderstood."

"This is the address you gave me, bro."

Ruzzo slid over to the window and looked up at the building. There was no mistaking the blocky plastic letters that ran along the roofline: Precious Acres. He paid the driver and walked up to the locked glass doors. The security desk in the lobby was unmanned and there was no intercom system anywhere in sight.

He pulled his phone out and called Maggie. She picked up just as a jumbo jet came in for a landing right overhead. Her headache-inducing voice cut through the din.

"Are you here?"

"Yes. I'm downstairs."

"Don't move. Somebody will come down to let you in."

He was watching through the glass doors five minutes later when the elevator opened and an attractive receptionist stepped out. She had long, curly hair that perfectly framed her high cheekbones and cinnamon skin. Any disappointment he felt about the Precious Acres corporate offices faded as she strutted through the lobby in a tight-fitting business suit to let him in.

"Thanks. My name's Tom Ruzzo, by the way."

"Yeah. No shit."

His head almost exploded when he heard her

voice. The mental image didn't jive with the super model standing in front of him.

"Maggie?"

"In the flesh. Come on, everybody's waiting for you upstairs."

"Whose everybody?"

They rode up in the elevator, she furiously texting on her phone and him in stunned silence. So far nothing about this trip was what he thought it would be. It was hard to judge how many more surprises he could take.

The doors slid open and she led him through a shabby office filled with empty cubicles. A few heads popped up here and there as they passed by, but there was an overwhelming stillness to the place that felt forsaken. The NYPD precinct where he used to work seemed like a nightclub in comparison, and that was saying a lot.

They eventually reached a door in the back corner. She gripped the handle and turned to face him with a grin.

"I hope you're ready for this."

She pushed the door open and stepped aside. He found himself in a massive boardroom with two identical conference tables side by side. Each table was twenty feet long and made of solid wood with high-backed leather chairs all the way around.

Rolf Kostbar was sitting at the head of the table on the right, accompanied by a handful of elderly business consultants and lawyers. His sister Heidi was similarly situated at the table on the left with her own group of trusted advisors. Both teams were embroiled in their own conversations, neither of them paying any attention to the other.

Maggie coughed and everybody looked up, clearly surprised they had visitors.

"Pardon the interruption. This is Tom Ruzzo, our Head of Security from Seatown. He just arrived. I knew you wanted to speak with him right away."

Maggie mouthed "good luck" to him and slipped out of the room, pulling the door shut behind her. Both groups reconvened their private huddles while Ruzzo waited for further instructions. It gave him time to study the two most powerful people in his world.

Rolf was broad-shouldered and doughy, with sandy brown hair that grew in a ring around the sides of his head. He had small, piggish eyes that were dull and lifeless behind designer glasses. A thin five o'clock shadow was forming on his round face, masking his permanently pursed lips and weak chin. He looked like a man who didn't sleep much.

Heidi was built from the same basic mold as her brother, but where he had given in to middle age she clearly worked hard to combat it. It was impossible for Ruzzo to tell if her sharp facial features and slim figure were the work of trainers or surgeons. That kind of dedication to youthfulness had to be all-consuming. The result was something sort of freakish, especially when the two of them were seated so close to each other.

Five minutes crawled by before Ruzzo's hangover caught up with him. He plopped down into the nearest seat, which happened to be at the end of Heidi Kostbar's table. Everybody at Rolf's table immediately stopped speaking when she finally addressed him, a smug look of victory on her face. Rolf and his team stood and filed out of the room.

"Thanks for joining us on such short notice, Mr. Ruzzo."

"Not a problem."

"I understand you've had some serious issues in Seatown over the last week."

"Yes...that's true. But I can assure you that I'm working closely with local law enforcement to remedy the situation."

A member of Heidi's team leaned in to whisper in her ear. She nodded a few times and said something quiet in response before the man went on. Ruzzo chanced a glance at Rolf's empty table, wondering where they had gone. Heidi jumped in again before he could form any real theories.

"I appreciate your dedication, but I wonder if the Seatown police are to be trusted with a case of this magnitude."

If she was trying to butter him up, it was working. But what could an aging debutante possibly know about Sgt. Badeaux's qualifications?

"Well, I'm not really sure what our options are. Unless there's something you aren't telling me."

She made eye contact with everybody seated near her at the table. There were nods all around before she went on.

"I want to remind you that you are here as an employee of Precious Acres. As such I expect that anything we discuss today will be kept in the strictest of confidence."

"Gotcha."

Now Heidi and her team stood and left the room without saying another word. It was less than a minute before Rolf's crew walked back in and took their seats. Ruzzo stayed put at Heidi's table, still trying to make sense of the situation. It wasn't until one of the grey haired advisors ventured a slight nod that Ruzzo finally got the picture.

He stood up and moved to a chair at the other table. Rolf started speaking the minute Ruzzo sat down.

"Thanks for joining us on such short notice, Mr. Ruzzo."

"Um, no problem."

"Do you know Randy Liddell?"

Ruzzo's eyes darted around the conference room, searching for the executive wet bar that surely must exist. He guessed it was built into the wall behind some secret panel, like in a spy movie. Probably right next to the torture chamber, considering what a freak show this place was.

"Not personally, but I know the name."

"We have reason to believe that he's involved in actively trying to sabotage Precious Acres, starting with our Seatown location. From there, we believe he plans to undermine the entire operation."

"You think he's killing our residents to put you out of business?"

"Suffice it to say that we believe he poses a very serious threat to our livelihood. Yours included."

"Is this just suspicion, or do you have proof?"

"Not as much as we would like, but we're hoping that proof will be irrelevant."

"Again. Why don't you just go to the police?"

Rolf conferred with his team. Ruzzo was starting to get seriously creeped out.

"Were you aware, Mr. Ruzzo, that Sgt. Badeaux was Randy Liddell's football coach? He's been like a father figure to Liddell since he was in grade school."

Son of a bitch.

That little sting operation of Sgt. Badeaux's probably wasn't a police case at all, but some sort of family feud. A wave of sickening anxiety washed over Ruzzo as he tried to consider what Shayna's role in all of this might be.

"And you think Sgt. Badeaux is in on this plot to destroy your business."

"We have no reason to believe that the police are involved in Mr. Liddell's plans, but we can't be sure who Sgt. Badeaux will side with if push comes to shove."

Ruzzo let out a nervous cough.

"What the hell do you expect me to do about that?"

"We are prepared to offer you a large sum of money for certain services outside of your current job description."

"Such as?"

"One million dollars to kill Randy Liddell."

"Wait. What?! You've got the wrong guy."

"Do we, Mr. Ruzzo? Take the night to think about it. You can contact me directly at this phone number tomorrow."

Rolf slid a business card across the table.

"But please don't mention our conversation to Ms. Walker. This situation has developed considerably since she invited you here yesterday. I'm sure you understand. It's for her own safety."

Ruzzo had one more question to ask. He knew it was now or never.

"Does this have anything to do with your brother Peter?"

"We aren't prepared to discuss personal family matters with you, Mr. Ruzzo. Thanks for your time. Think very seriously about our offer."

Rolf brought his hands up onto the table, just as Heidi and her team returned. Everybody in the room was silent as Ruzzo slipped out.

Maggie was waiting for him when he left the boardroom. Something about her seemed to have softened. Ruzzo could barely contain himself.

"Christ. Once a circus, always a circus."

"Keep your voice down."

She took him by the wrist and they ducked into an unoccupied office.

"They haven't spoken in years. Neither of them will even acknowledge the other's existence, except in legal documents."

"Why didn't you tell me?"

"It's something you have to see to believe. I'm just glad that somebody else knows what I'm going through now."

"Why don't you just quit?"

"Velvet handcuffs. They pay me twice what I would make anywhere else."

"What about the bankruptcy?"

"You saw all the empty cubicles out there."

As a low-level employee himself Ruzzo's ego should have been bruised, but he accepted the way the world worked. Everybody has their place. People like Maggie made an obscene amount of money to babysit eccentric millionaires. People like him only got ahead if they were willing to kill the company's enemies.

"Come on. Let's continue our conversation on the way to the terminal."

The elevator ride back down was the exact opposite of the ride up. Maggie spoke the whole time, thoughts flying from her mouth as they formed. He took it all in, listening closely as they walked through the lobby and across the parking lot. There weren't any new revelations, just more details about the company and how she thought each of them fit into it.

"Who knows? They could name you VP of Security for the entire operation."

"That position doesn't even exist."

"Not yet, but it might one day. You and I should stick together."

She hit the alarm button on her keychain and a late model SUV blinked to life. Ruzzo noticed there was no baby seat in the back. They both climbed in and she started the engine. The top button of her blouse was undone and he could see the lacy outline of her bra. It was amazing how little her voice bothered him now.

"So, who's your prime suspect in the murders?"

If that was a test, it was pretty weak.

"It isn't really my case, but I've got some theories."

"Anything you care to share?"

"Not really. Like I said, just theories at this point."

"I see how it's going to be."

Ruzzo laughed. He wanted to trust her, but Rolf had been pretty clear about keeping her in the dark. And Mr. Adamoli's crossword puzzle theory was too hard to explain in such a short drive. He countered with a question of his own.

"What do you know about Peter, the third triplet?"

She kept her gaze on the road, but almost spit out her response.

"Ha! I see you've been talking to Billy Randolph."

"Seatown's pretty small. It was only a matter of time until I met him."

"Take my word for it, once Billy's got your attention he'll never leave you alone. He's a little off his rocker."

"You didn't answer the question."

The car swerved as she shook her head and laughed.

"It's no big secret. They had a brother and he died. End of story."

"What about all the paternity claims? That has to be costing them a pretty penny."

"Maybe a few years ago, but nobody has come forward recently."

Ruzzo knew he only had a minute left before the ride ended. He intended to make the most of their time together, especially now that she seemed to consider him an ally.

"I just don't understand why they would care. The guy's been dead for twenty years. These people can't possibly have any real claim to Precious Acres, right?"

"You would think, but every corporation is set up differently. This one just happens to be very family focused."

"Meaning what? There has to be an heir to hand the business down to?"

"There doesn't have to be..."

"...but if there is a legitimate claim, then the heir becomes a full partner."

"Crazy, right?"

Maggie got a call from Heidi Kostbar just as they arrived at the passenger-loading zone. The traffic cops started blowing their whistles before Ruzzo even opened his door to step out. Both of them were too distracted to say goodbye. She was gone before he reached the sidewalk.

EDITOR

The *Sentinel* crossword puzzle was the first thing on Ruzzo's mind when he woke up in the morning. He considered getting a subscription so he could stop stealing from his neighbors, but decided against it. Mr. Adamoli seemed a lot less credible now that Ruzzo knew some of the residents were volunteering at the paper.

He went downstairs and surveyed the landscape through the window before opening the front door. There was no sign of his bike-riding tormentors, but that was no guarantee of safety. It felt ridiculous to be cowering in fear over a few teenagers when he was on the verge of becoming a professional hit man.

Or was he? There was so much to consider. He was glad it was his day off.

The bricks outside felt cool against his bare feet. He was bending down to pick up the newspaper when ice-cold water dumped from a bucket mounted overhead. Ruzzo was drenched from head to toe and shivering with rage when he heard the teens laughing.

He took off at a sprint. The three boys hesitated

for a second, unsure of what to do next. It was as if they never considered the possibility that they might get caught. Ruzzo had almost reached them before they finally started pedaling for their lives. The slowest one was only a few feet in front of Ruzzo's outstretched hand when he downshifted and picked up speed. Ruzzo staggered to a stop, picking up a rock from the ground. He threw it with his remaining strength and watched it buzz by the smallest kid's ear.

In that moment he knew for certain that his days as Head of Security were over. Luckily, he had options.

He was in his apartment and completely naked once again as he opened the wet newspaper and read the first clue. "They fix syntax." The answer was six letters long. His computer dinged before he could try to solve it. Another email from Shayna was waiting.

Sorry I ran out on you again. I didn't have a choice. You'll be happier without me.
xoxo, me

He could read her desperation between the lines. His response was short and sweet, but he meant every word.

Call me. You always have a choice.

Ruzzo hit refresh again and again while he waited for her reply. It was several minutes before it finally came through.

He would kill us both.

His phone rang as he frantically typed his next response. He lunged to answer it, relieved that she had come to her senses and decided to call.

"Meet me down at the station."

"What? Why?"

Sgt. Badeaux hung up without responding. His tone had been neutral, so it was hard to gauge what this might be about. Ruzzo knew he needed to be prepared for almost anything, especially considering the information he was given yesterday.

He retyped his last message to Shayna, settling in the end for the two most important words: "Call me." There was no way to understand what she was going through, but he wanted her to know that he would always be there for her.

When no response came after five long minutes, Ruzzo turned his attention back to Sgt. Badeaux. He was planning to spend the day at the beach anyway, so he shoved a bathing suit and beach towel into his backpack. The Smith & Wesson revolver went in last. Ruzzo pulled on a pair of shorts, a T-shirt and flip-flops before heading downtown.

Nobody was at the police station when he arrived. He sat down in a chair to wait and saw the *Sentinel* crossword sitting there. The answer to one across was filled in: EDITOR.

Ruzzo was kicking himself for not getting that one, until it clicked. He got up and ran out the door in the direction of the newspaper office. Sgt. Badeaux and his posse were milling around outside when Ruzzo arrived.

"I thought you'd know where to find us."

"Is Randolph okay?"

"I'm afraid not. Friend of yours?"

"Not exactly. We only met a couple of days ago. Is he dead?"

"Damn near. Come with me."

Sgt. Badeaux opened the door and Ruzzo followed him inside. Something felt wrong from the moment they entered. Randolph's limp body was being carefully loaded onto a gurney by a couple of paramedics. His face looked like a purple balloon, swollen and bruised beyond recognition. Spots of blood dotted the blanket that covered him and his right arm was bent at an odd angle. Ruzzo stepped aside as they wheeled him by, the rage already twisting his guts.

"Is he going to make it?"

Sgt. Badeaux never took his reflective gaze off of Ruzzo's face.

"No telling. We think he was investigating the murders."

"Did he at least figure out who did it?"

"Funny you should ask. He was clutching this microcassette recorder in his hand when we found him."

Sgt. Badeaux handed it over. Ruzzo was impressed with how consistent he was when it came to mishandling evidence.

"Go ahead, give a listen."

Ruzzo heard his own voice on the playback.

...I killed those people.

"I can explain."

"I guess you probably should."

Ruzzo was very aware of the extra weight in his backpack when the officers took it from him. They led him outside to a bus bench. His heart was racing as he tried to construct a version of the story that proved his innocence. He also had to explain the gun. It wasn't going to be easy.

Sgt. Badeaux strolled over a couple minutes later and sat next to him. He set the backpack down between them.

"Let me guess. That was just a snippet from a longer conversation."

"How did you know?"

"That crazy son of a bitch tried recording everything I said for the last twenty years. I lost count of the times I had to turn his damned recorder off."

"So you know I didn't kill anybody?"

"I only met you a few days ago, but I don't think you've killed anybody in Florida. At least not yet."

The comment caught Ruzzo off guard. Was it possible that Sgt. Badeaux knew about the Kostbar's contract on Randy Liddell? His parting shot didn't make it any clearer.

"Enjoy the beach, Ruzzo. Don't do anything stupid with that gun of yours."

Mikey was walking out of the Rusty Pelican as Ruzzo walked in. Bars that opened up first thing in the morning served a vital public service as far as both of them were concerned.

"Tommy! You're here a little early."

"Day off. Where are you heading?"

"Taking Cavanaugh out for some deep sea fishing. You should come along, if you don't already have plans."

Ruzzo didn't have to think it over for very long. A little time out on the ocean might help clear his head before he called Tampa. He already wanted Randy Liddell dead for the way he was treating Shayna, so he might as well get paid for it.

"You mind if I get a drink first?"

"Knock yourself out. Boat leaves in a half hour. I'll meet you down at the dock."

It's amazing how many drinks you can squeeze into thirty minutes when you put our mind to it. Without Mikey around Ruzzo could really concentrate on the task at hand. He was halfway through his third cocktail twenty minutes later when a tall man with a waxed moustache wandered into the bar. He motioned to the stool next to Ruzzo, speaking in a silky Southern drawl.

"You mind?"

This joker would be right at home in Brooklyn if it weren't for that accent.

"It's a free country."

The man gave a soft groan when he climbed up to take a seat, as if he was dealing with an injury. A young bartender that Ruzzo didn't recognize came over and set a can of beer down on the bar without a word. The stranger sitting next to him placed an envelope beside it. The man nodded as the bartender swiped the envelope into his apron with a fluid motion. Ruzzo watched the interaction from the corner of his eye, sure that he just witnessed a sloppy drug deal. As usual, he couldn't stop himself from speaking up.

"Pretty slick. You might want to do that somewhere a little more private next time."

The man spun to face Ruzzo, clearly sizing him up.

"You should probably mind your own business, little man."

"What'd you call me?"

Ruzzo jumped up and kicked his stool across the floor. The man beside him didn't even flinch as he stood up and threw some cash on the bar.

"You New Yorkers are always picking fights that you can't win."

"Oh yeah? Try me, son."

"Maybe next time."

The man turned and limped out of the bar. Ruzzo watched him leave before grabbing his untouched beer and drinking it down.

Ruzzo, Cavanaugh and Mikey were two miles out at sea and spread around the bobbing boat. Cavanaugh had already reeled in a black grouper weighing in at over thirty pounds. Mikey was in the cabin cleaning the fish to cook part of it for lunch.

The sweltering midday sun was beating down on the boat. Diesel exhaust and the smell of fresh bait were really getting to Ruzzo. He sidled along the rail toward Cavanaugh who quickly stepped away.

"That's close enough. I don't want you getting our lines tangled."

"That was an impressive catch. I take it you've done a lot of fishing."

"Hard not to, growing up around here. I bet the

only thing you'd catch off of Manhattan these days is the clap."

"Funny."

"If you say so, Bubba."

Cavanaugh took a few steps toward the bow. Ruzzo followed, feeling a little queasy from the motion of the boat.

"Mikey said you used to be a comedian."

"Sounds like Mikey needs to keep his trap shut."

"Come on. What's the big secret?"

Cavanaugh raised an eyebrow and snorted. Ruzzo could see that the groundskeeper was trying to decide how much personal information to share.

"There ain't much to tell. I was just a stupid kid who followed his dreams, and it led me smack into a brick wall. So I came back home with my tail between my legs."

Ruzzo wanted to mention the open mic night, but knew that one of them would end up swimming back to shore if he did.

"Did you ever make it to New York?"

"More times than I'd care to remember."

Cavanaugh squinted his eyes hard, studying the horizon. Ruzzo gave it a moment before he went on.

"Well, it's too bad I missed you at The Rusty Pelican. I'd like to see you perform."

"Play your cards right and you just might one day."

Cavanaugh brought the rod up and cast his line with a flick of the wrist. The reel whizzed as the hook and bait disappeared in the distance.

"Since we're sharing, let me ask you a question. How'd you get mixed up with Shayna Billups?"

"We met at the police station in Queens."

"No shit. What did they bring her in for?"

"Assaulting an officer."

"So, of course you asked her out. Ain't that how *Romeo and Juliet* starts?"

"I'm not sure, but I'm hoping our story has a happier ending."

"I bet. Speaking of happy endings, you got any info about the murders? There's some pretty scared residents over at Precarious Acres these days."

Now it was Ruzzo's turn to choose his words carefully.

"Nothing you can't read in the paper."

"Huh."

"What?"

"I just assumed an experienced NYPD cop could teach a good old boy like Sgt. Badeaux a lesson or two. But I guess that's why you ain't a cop no more."

Ruzzo took a couple of uneven steps forward, doing his best to be threatening although his head was swimming.

"For your information, I could run circles around that clown. I already gave him the best lead he's gotten in this case."

"Well, I guess that makes you a deputy clown."

"You're hilarious, Cavanaugh."

"If you say so, Bubba."

Ruzzo slid the end of his rod into a holder mounted on the rail and headed for the cabin. The boat lurched as two rolling swells came up underneath them. He needed to lie down, or puke, or get another drink. Probably all three.

Mikey looked up when Ruzzo walked in. He was adding a splash of white wine to the fish in the pan. Ruzzo dry heaved at the smell, but managed to take a seat at the dinette without letting anything come up.

"You look like shit."

"I'll be fine. What the hell's up with Cavanaugh today?"

"No telling. He's been acting funny since that open mic night. I actually planned this fishing trip as a sort of apology for talking him into it."

"Well, he doesn't have to be an asshole to me. I wasn't even there that night."

Ruzzo pulled his phone out to see if Shayna had emailed, but he got zero reception that far out to sea. Mikey was walking over to set a cocktail down when something caught his attention through the window.

"Oh shit. Here we go!"

He dashed from the cabin. Ruzzo took a big gulp from the glass and followed.

Mikey was pointing down at the ocean where a pod of dolphins were leaping from the water on the starboard side of the boat. Cavanaugh's clothes were piled on the deck, but he was nowhere to be seen. Ruzzo took a few tentative steps and peeked over the rail.

The groundskeeper popped up out of the water like a cork and started swimming hard for the nearest dolphin. He'd only gotten a few yards from the boat when two more dolphins swam up under him.

Ruzzo ran into the cabin and pulled the Smith & Wesson from his backpack. He was back at the rail a moment later, trying to level the weapon at the tilting horizon. It had been a few months since he last went to the shooting range, but he was pretty sure he could still hit a moving target.

Cavanaugh was really thrashing around now. It might already be too late. Mikey didn't see what Ruzzo was doing right next to him until the last second.

"Whoa! Are you crazy?"

He pushed the gun to the side and pointed out to the waves. Ruzzo's jaw almost hit the deck when he saw that Cavanaugh was actually splashing and swimming with the wild mammals. He was filled with awe for a brief moment before his knees gave out beneath him.

Ruzzo woke up to the sound of a chugging motor. The late afternoon sun was roasting him through the cabin window. He sat up on the bench and found Cavanaugh seated nearby, drinking a cup of coffee.

"Rise and shine, Ahab."

"Jesus. How long was I out?"

"Just about an hour. You always carry a big gun around?"

Ruzzo's head was pounding and his tongue felt like it was coated with sandpaper.

"Just since the murders."

"Can't say I blame you."

"Are we almost back to shore?"

"Fifteen more minutes."

Cavanaugh stood up to look out the window. A thin sliver of land was visible on the horizon now.

"You aren't thinking of going after Randy Liddell with that gun, are you?"

"I'd have to find him first."

"Have you tried looking at his place over near Brockton Beach? He's lived there as long as I can remember."

"Thanks for the tip."

"It's your funeral. Just let me now if you need back up."

"Back up? You've got to be kidding. I can handle that hick on my own."

"If you say so, Bubba."

"That's another thing. Why do you keep calling me 'Bubba?'"

"It's just a nickname we use down here. Don't mean any offense by it."

Ruzzo talk a deep breath and tried to calm down. If Cavanaugh noticed, he didn't care.

"You ever even met Randy Liddell?"

"Nope."

"You should look him up sometime. He was an all-state quarterback back in high school. Got a full ride scholarship to a college up north. He's not exactly a typical 'hick.'"

"Seriously?"

"Probably would have gone pro too, if he didn't get injured his junior year."

"Thanks. I'll look into it."

"Least I could do for the guy who tried to save me from those evil dolphins."

It didn't take much digging on the Internet to get info about Randy Liddell. Practically every Florida newspaper from a decade ago was writing about the college football star with the bright future. The pictures were much more troubling than the facts.

All this time Ruzzo had assumed that Randy Liddell was a small time, local yokel pusher. What he found instead was a six-foot-two, all-American poster boy with blue eyes, feathered hair and big white teeth. Ruzzo couldn't find any recent pictures, but he already knew what Liddell looked like these days. They had almost gotten into a fight at The Rusty Pelican earlier that morning.

Ruzzo's blood boiled as he read through a decade-old article about his rival.

STAR QUARTERBACK INJURED IN BAR FIGHT

Former Florida all-state quarterback and Seatown native Randy Liddell was arrested last night following a brawl at a Seatown bar. The twenty-one-year-old is accused of assaulting another patron with a beer bottle while on spring break from college in New York.

The fight started when Liddell found the victim dancing with his date, twenty-two-year-old Seatown resident, Shayna Billups. Following the beer bottle incident, witnesses say that several of the victim's friends "attacked Liddell, punching and kicking him for several minutes" before throwing him down a flight of stairs. Liddell was rushed to the hospital where he was treated for a broken wrist and multiple leg fractures. Seatown police took Liddell into custody shortly after he was released from the hospital.

The injuries didn't just end his season, but his entire career. And just like that, Randy Liddell slipped from the Florida spotlight and almost completely off the grid. All Ruzzo could find were a couple of police blotter reports from the following years. It seemed that Liddell had gotten addicted to painkillers during his recovery and ended up dealing himself. The only other time Shayna Billups was mentioned is in connection with a domestic violence report in the *Seatown Sentinel*.

Ruzzo was filled with a mixture of jealousy and rage as he reached for his phone.

"I was hoping you would call. Do we have a deal?"

"Three million."

"Come on, Mr. Ruzzo—"

"The number only goes up if we negotiate."

"Okay, but if the number changes than so do some of the conditions."

"I'll be the judge of that."

"From now on you only take orders from me."

"Meaning no more contact with Maggie Walker?"

"Or anybody else you might have had contact with at our Tampa offices."

"Heidi."

"Let's just say my partner isn't as liberal with money as I am. I'm afraid that if she finds out about the sum we've agreed on, I'll be forced to cancel our agreement. When can I expect the job to be completed?"

"When the time is right."

"The clock's ticking, Mr. Ruzzo."

MURDER

Ruzzo didn't have to go down to get the *Sentinel* the next morning. It was sitting on the bed right next to him when he rolled over. He opened his eyes and saw that one across was already filled in: MURDER.

The image of Billy Randolph's mangled body was haunting his thoughts as he tried to clear his sleepy mind. He desperately wanted to have a chat with the old newspaper editor as soon the doctor's would let him.

That paranoid bastard must have figured something out about the murders, and it almost got him killed.

"Good morning, Mr. Ruzzo."

He would recognize that voice anywhere. Ruzzo propped himself up until he was sitting cross-legged on the mattress. His naked body was barely concealed under the covers. Mr. Adamoli was seated in a chair across from the bed, Ruzzo's Smith & Wesson in his lap.

"That's twice you've broken in here now and stolen my gun. I'd snap your neck if you weren't so fucking old."

"Save your idle threats. Do you have any news to share?"

"Maybe, but do you mind if I take a piss first?"

He rolled to the floor and walked to the bathroom, knowing that a good Catholic was always more offended by nudity than murder. It was the least he could do to thank Mr. Adamoli for the intrusion. The old man hadn't moved an inch when Ruzzo returned wearing a robe.

"You still here?"

"You can get rid of me very easily. Just tell me what you know."

"Or you'll shoot me?"

Ruzzo wasn't so sure of the answer himself. There was a slight edge to his unexpected guest that hadn't been there the last time they spoke. A sort of manic energy that intensified when he played with the gun.

"I've lost a few friends in the past week. You'll have to forgive my impatience."

"Fair enough. Unfortunately, the only real lead I had is in coma."

"Yes. Poor Billy. I always assumed his curiosity would get the best of him."

Mr. Adamoli looked like he had aged a decade in the course of their conversation. His circle of friends had gotten pretty small. He was almost completely alone in Florida these days. Ruzzo could relate.

"Give me a couple more days. I think I can put an end to all of this."

"That's what I've been waiting to hear."

Ruzzo opened the door and watched his guest slowly descend the stairs. The phone started ringing the moment he was back inside the apartment. He slumped down into a chair and picked up the receiver.

"Ruzzo."

Nobody spoke, but he could hear yelling in the background. His mind went straight to Shayna and Liddell.

"Who is this?"

"It's Maggie."

Her voice was almost bearable when she spoke in a whisper.

"Everything all right?"

"Rolf and Heidi have been screaming at each other for almost an hour. I had to send the staff home early. It sounds like they're going to kill each other."

"Just call the police. There's no way I'll make it there in time to do anything."

"I'm not calling for help, idiot. I've got something to tell you."

"Shoot."

Ruzzo cringed at his own choice of words. It was hard to know if he should be playing Head of Security, ex-cop, or hit man. Between the unexpected phone call and Rolf's demands for secrecy, he was starting to get a little paranoid.

"She keeps screaming your name over and over."

"Heidi? Why?"

"I can't really hear everything. It's something about you and a lot of money. Did you get a raise that I don't know about?"

Ruzzo heard a loud crash, like metal garbage cans being thrown down subway stairs. Whatever was happening at the Precious Acres corporate offices, it wasn't good. Maggie went from a whisper to an ear-splitting shout in a heartbeat.

"Oh shit! I gave to go—"

"No! Maggie, wait!"

His phone went dead. It was time to go earn three million dollars.

Ruzzo drove his golf cart to the highway and headed out of town. A steady flow of pickup trucks blew by him in the swampy no man's land. The passengers hurled beer bottles and insults as they passed. He kept to the shoulder, watching the egrets fly between the Bay Trees. It was almost twenty minutes before he saw the unmarked turn off for Brockton Beach. He reached over and opened the glove compartment to make sure that the Smith & Wesson was still there.

He had only been here once before, for a kinky

sunset walk with Shayna. Her love of public sex was something he never understood. Somehow she still always managed to convince him.

The golf cart's wheels bumped along on the muddy, gravel road. Hand painted real estate signs and the occasional mailbox popped up, but no houses were visible through the thick overgrowth. It was the kind of place that looked like Mayberry during the daytime and *Deliverance* at night. The temperature dropped a few degrees as Ruzzo drove deeper into the shadows.

He could hear the waves breaking on the beach when the gravel finally gave way to sand. The little red convertible came into view before the house did. He hid the golf cart in a stand of trees and grabbed the gun.

Ruzzo followed the edge of the road, keeping one eye on the house as he walked. He ducked down behind the convertible and listened. Classic rock was playing somewhere inside the house. He guessed it was probably Skynyrd. Or maybe The Allman Brothers? He never really could tell the difference.

It definitely ain't Sinatra or Jay-Z.

He peeked around the front fender to see if the coast was clear along the perimeter of the house. It was a massive structure, two stories tall and bursting with porches and balconies. The exterior had been whitewashed many years ago, but the yellowing paint was chipped and peeling now. Large patches of the roof were covered in mismatched shingles and several windows were cracked on the lower floor.

Ruzzo scurried through the knee-high grass that grew in clumps across the yard. His back was pressed up against the rear of the house and the gun was pointed at the ground. The windows on either side of him seemed to be covered with plastic trash bags from the inside. He was starting to wonder if Randy and Shayna were running a meth lab when the water heater sputtered to life right next to him. He jumped at the sound.

It took him a moment to regain his senses. Somebody was doing the dishes or taking a shower. Either way, this might be his best chance to sneak inside.

The steps leading up to the front porch creaked under his feet as he headed for the front door. Two tattered and musty couches sat under the darkened windows that once overlooked the beach. He pulled the screen door open and tested the knob. It swung in silently. He was soon standing inside of the mudroom.

Dirty leather boots and bright red high heels were lying side by side on the scuffed linoleum floor. The wallpaper was peeling down from the ceiling like tiny crashing waves. There was a closed door in each of the three remaining walls of the suffocating space.

Ruzzo pulled the first one open and discovered a closet stacked high with water damaged moving boxes. The second door was locked. His remaining option was in the wall right in front of him. He turned the knob and gave a push. The music got louder as he stepped through heavy velvet curtains and into an impressive plantation house.

The polished wooden floors were dotted with pieces of handcrafted furniture and antique rugs. Enormous family portraits hung from the walls, their muted colors casting an unnatural glow in the dusty air. A sweeping staircase lined the wall on the right and led up to a second story landing. Tiny birds were chirping and darting from the bannister to the massive chandelier overhead.

Ruzzo was so busy taking it all in that he almost didn't notice the music had stopped. He leapt to his right and ducked behind a curving sofa. Shayna came down the staircase a moment later with wet hair, an escort on either side of her. Ruzzo's heart started racing as he ventured a peek at Randy Liddell. He had one hand on Shayna's lower back and was nervously twirling his moustache with the other.

The man on her right was much easier to identify because of his mirrored sunglasses and trooper hat.

Sgt. Badeaux was doing most of the talking as they reached the lower floor.

"I understand your concern, but don't do anything rash."

Shayna gave Liddell a worried look as he responded.

"That's easy for you to say since you're not the one in the crosshairs."

"Well, you can always disappear for a while. That's kind of your specialty."

"Last I checked this was still America. I come and go as I please. Why don't you do your job and put an end to all of this?"

"Take it easy, Randy. I'm working on it, but I need some real proof first. My job is to uphold the law."

"'Real proof'? You and I both know this has nothing to do with the law. What happened to that lead you said you had?"

"It didn't pan out, but we're still working on it."

They had reached the velvet curtains and were on their way out the door. Ruzzo scooted around to the side of the sofa, gripping the Smith & Wesson tight.

"If anybody lays a finger on you, they'll have to answer to me."

"Yeah, well, I just hope you aren't too late. Come on, I'll drop you off at your car on my way out of town."

Ruzzo didn't exhale until he heard the red convertible start. He had just enough time to take a deep breath before the front door clicked shut. Shayna's perfume seemed to fill the room now that it was just the two of them. She passed by the sofa, speaking out loud. Her voiced echoed in the empty room as she walked.

"I guess it's just me, all alone in this big scary house now."

She reached the base of the staircase.

"All by myself for the rest of the afternoon."

He could her hear her padding up to the landing.

"I guess I'll just go climb into bed and hide under the covers."

Ruzzo rose up to venture a peek. A trail of her clothes led from the front door to the base of the stairs. He just caught a glimpse of her naked body as she took the top step and turned the corner out of view.

She was curled up next to him an hour later, huffing and puffing in the four-poster bed. Ruzzo was gently tracing the firm curves of her new boobs with the tips of his fingers. It was hard not to think about Liddell when he looked at them. His blood started boiling when he spotted the bruises all over her ribs and legs.

"Does it hurt?"

"Don't flatter yourself!"

She giggled and smacked his chest. Ruzzo rolled his eyes.

"I meant the surgery."

"What, these? I thought the liposuction was much worse."

"Jesus. How many procedures have you had done?"

"A few. Of course, most of the fat from the lipo went back here."

She gave her own ass a little slap. Ruzzo had to admit that the doctor who created that masterpiece was a true artist.

"That's a pretty expensive habit you've created for yourself."

"Take a look around. I'm not paying for any of this, at least not with money."

"Shayna—"

"I'm fine, baby. I can leave any time I want."

He let his eyes wander across the room, trying to control his welling rage.

"Where did he get all this money anyway?"

"Let's not talk about him right now."

"You brought it up. Come on, I want to know."

She rolled onto her back and gave a long, slow sigh.

"Whatever it is ain't legal. He's gone all hours of the night, and days at a time. I'm not expecting to see him again until tomorrow afternoon."

Somehow Ruzzo knew he wouldn't feel as bad about killing a scumbag dealer.

"You can leave whenever you want. Come stay with me again."

"I know that, Tommy, but I still love him. That's a shitty thing to say when I'm laying here naked with you, but it's the truth."

Shayna might as well have stood up and crushed his nuts with her heel. She reached over and tweaked his nipple.

"Isn't there something more fun we could be doing?"

"What were the three of you chatting about on the stairs earlier?"

"Oh that? Randy can be a little paranoid. He called Bob over because he thinks somebody's trying to kill him. I think about it myself sometimes."

Ruzzo had never thought to ask what Sgt. Badeaux's first name was before. Bob Badeaux sounded like some kind of voodoo incantation as he repeated it in his head.

"Did he say who was trying to kill him?"

She brought her leg over his and rolled up to straddle him. He knew he wouldn't be getting any more information out of her now, but he was okay with the alternative. They still had a whole night ahead before Liddell got home.

"Hey. How did you know I was hiding behind the sofa downstairs earlier?"

She buried her head in his neck and took a deep breath.

"Oh, baby. I could smell you."

BASH

Ruzzo was sitting alone in a booth at Sodee's. The *Sentinel* was spread out in front of him. A cup of warm coffee was holding down one of the corners, a piece of key lime pie on another. The clue for one across was "Big party." He filled in the answer and set his pen down: BASH.

Sgt. Badeaux would be arriving for their meeting any minute now. Ruzzo had to find out the real reason that the Seatown Police wanted him to get information about Randy Liddell. He thought it was best for them to meet in public, in case the answer came in the form of a bullet.

"Breakfast of champions."

Ruzzo looked up and saw the mirrored sunglasses above him. He pointed to the pie and told his guest to help himself. Sgt. Badeaux patted his belly before sitting down.

"Too early for me. Is the crossword hard today?"

"I'm actually getting pretty good at it."

"I bet. Although I'm still not convinced you're getting anything out of it."

"That might be true. Did you ever interview Mr. Adamoli?"

"Just spoke with him a couple days ago. He's a little intense."

"You can say that again. You think he's involved?"

"We're considering all possibilities. But I don't think he's some kind of mafia mastermind, if that's what you're asking."

"What about Mr. Geratti's nephew?"

"He never showed up. Body's been on ice down at the morgue ever since you guys found it."

"Christ. Getting old seems like a nightmare."

"You ain't kidding, but it's inevitable. Unless you check out young."

Sgt. Badeaux brought his hands up and set them on the table in plain sight.

"Why did you ask me to meet you here, Ruzzo?"

"I wanted to see if you needed any more help with the Shayna Billups investigation."

"We've got it under control, but thanks."

"Well, I hope she's at least off the suspect list for the murders now."

"Nothing changes until we have somebody in custody."

Ruzzo brought his hands down on the table. Coffee sloshed over the rim of his mug.

"What's that supposed to mean?"

"Shayna Billups is hell on wheels. Nobody

knows that better than Randy Liddell."

"Like he's some upstanding citizen. I swear to God, the way you idolize high school football players down here is disgusting."

"Now you listen to me. That kid wasn't just some local football hero. He worked his ass off to rise above the hand he was dealt."

"Which was what, exactly?"

"Let's just say that his mother had drug problems of her own. She was a real pretty girl, but a screw came loose once Randy was born."

"What about his father?"

"It was just the two of them in that big old house. She had boyfriends now and again, but every one of them was a raging alcoholic who beat the tar out of Randy for fun. I used to think that's how he got so good at dodging rushers."

Even Ruzzo had to admit that Liddell had it pretty rough growing up.

"That's awful."

"It certainly wasn't paradise. I have to admit I was pretty relieved when she finally passed away last year."

"Was it an overdose?"

"Autopsy was inconclusive, but it was the drugs that did her in one way or another. It's just a crying shame to see Randy following in her footsteps. Nothing was ever the same for that boy once Shayna came into his life."

"So she has it coming because he never got to play pro football? He's the monster here, not her."

"Sounds like Randy's career isn't the only one she's responsible for ending."

Their argument was cut short when a muffled voice started barking at Sgt. Badeaux from the radio on his belt. He reached down and set it on the table between them.

"Sergeant, are you there? Copy."

He pressed the button on the side to respond.

"Go for Badeaux."

"There's been another murder. All units en route to the crime scene. Over."

Sgt. Badeaux and Ruzzo jumped to their feet in unison.

Mr. Fava's lifeless body was sprawled out across the floor of the Precious Acres gazebo. A folding chessboard was right beside him, the black and white plastic pieces scattered all around. His heavy cane was covered in blood and carefully laid out across his chest. The space between his straw hat and the collar of his shirt was a fleshy pile of chunky goo.

Sgt. Badeaux parked his car and Ruzzo followed him up the concrete path. They stepped over a few mountain bikes as they walked. The responding officers had three teenagers handcuffed and sitting on the grass. All of them had puffy, bloodshot eyes and identical bewildered expressions on their freckled faces.

"What do we have here?"

"We arrived and found these three kids fleeing from the scene. One of them had the victim's wallet in his possession when we caught up to them."

"Interesting. You're Tammy Fitzpatrick's boys, right?"

They all nodded in unison. Sgt. Badeaux knelt down in front of the oldest brother.

"Did you little fuck wads kill this man?"

"No, sir."

"Did you see who did?"

"No, sir."

"You sure? Because if I find out you're lying to me you'll be picking up soap in a prison shower for the rest of your life."

"Yes, sir. I mean, I'm not lying. I didn't see who did it. Can we go home now?"

"Hell no."

Sgt. Badeaux stood up, discharging a long string of brown tobacco juice in the process. He hiked up his belt and walked over to the nearest officer.

"Take these boys down to the station to get a statement, but put them in separate cells. Let's see if their story changes any when you've got them alone. And for God's sake, don't take them home until they sober up. Their momma would have a heart attack if she knew they were smoking weed and stealing from dead people."

Ruzzo bit his tongue. He knew these were the kids that had been tormenting him, and he would love to see them raked over the coals, but even he was convinced of their innocence. It was a big leap from tossing a few eggs to beating a man's head in. They probably discovered Mr. Fava when they were riding by and decided that he wouldn't miss his wallet. Weed wasn't cheap in this part of Florida, and there were no part time jobs for juvenile delinquents.

Sgt. Badeaux turned his attention to the body.

"What's missing, Ruzzo?"

"His head."

"Very funny. I was talking about the evidence."

It didn't take long to solve this one.

"There's no crossword puzzle."

"Our killer is getting sloppy."

"And more violent."

Ruzzo stopped by Mr. Adamoli's condo after he left the crime scene. He wanted to be the one who told him about Mr. Fava, mostly to see his reaction. It was still hard to tell what his role in all of this was.

There was no Sinatra music to greet Ruzzo when he approached the door this time. He knocked lightly at first, finally increasing the volume when nobody answered. The door cracked open. Ruzzo stuck his head inside and called out. There was still no response so he stepped inside.

It took a moment for his eyes to adjust to the darkness. The place had been completely ransacked. Mr. Adamoli was nowhere to be found.

Ruzzo tore out the front door and went back to find Sgt. Badeaux. He had to tell him that there might be a second crime scene.

There was an email waiting from Shayna when Ruzzo finally got home late that night. The police had searched Mr. Adamoli's apartment, and the entire grounds of Precious Acres throughout the afternoon. There was no way to know what happened to him, but Ruzzo wasn't holding his breath for a happy ending.

He was feeling pretty overwhelmed by the whole situation and ready to drink himself to sleep. The thought even crossed his mind to just trash Shayna's message without opening it. They had no hope for a future together and he wasn't in the mood for any more drama, no matter how great the sex was.

His finger was hovering over the delete button when he realized that the email had an attachment. He had a pretty good idea what it might be.

Nobody gave video tours of their body quite like she did.

Ruzzo stood up to pour himself a drink. The computer was beckoning to him across the room, but he intended to savor the anticipation. Unfortunately, the alcohol was having no effect on his exhausted mind.

He made his way back over and clicked on the video file. She had totally outdone herself. It wasn't just a smartphone video of Shayna teasing the camera. This was high quality security footage from their recent afternoon in bed together.

I can't believe she was recording us that whole time.

He watched for a few seconds before scrolling down to read her message.

> *Enjoy it while you can. That's the last time you will ever see her alive.*
>
> *—RL*

Ruzzo nearly tipped over backwards in his chair trying to stand up. He struggled to put his shoes on and rushed to the door, realizing at the last moment that he'd forgotten his gun. Their heavy breathing and moaning was still playing in the background when he raced out into the hallway.

He rounded the corner at the bottom of the stairs and ran straight into Cavanaugh. The groundskeeper fell back into the bank of mailboxes with a loud crash and slid to the floor. Ruzzo reached out to help him up. Cavanaugh was slurring his words.

"Got a hot date?"

Ruzzo needed back up if he was going to rescue Shayna, but he didn't know how much information to share. He settled on a lie.

"Randy beat the shit out of Shayna. She just called me."

"Hitting women is chicken shit. Somebody ought to teach him a lesson."

"That's what I had in mind. I could use a hand in case things get out of control."

"They at his place?"

"That's where I'm heading."

"Hm. You got your gun?"

"I do."

"Good. We're gonna need it."

Cavanaugh almost tumbled out of the golf cart on their first few turns. Ruzzo finished the ride down the highway with one hand on the steering wheel and the other twisted tight around his passenger's collar. They were turning onto the dirt road when Ruzzo smelled smoke. A red and orange glow was lighting up the trees in the distance as they approached the beach.

Randy Liddell's house was completely engulfed in flames when they arrived. They couldn't get too close because of the intense heat. The red convertible was still parked out front. Ruzzo knew Shayna might still be inside, but there was absolutely nothing he could do to save her.

Ruzzo fell to his knees and started sobbing in the dirt. Cavanaugh plopped down beside him, putting his massive hand on Ruzzo's back.

"All you can do tonight is pray."

ASHES

Sgt. Badeaux was doing the crossword puzzle when Ruzzo entered his office the next morning. It was clear that neither of them had slept thanks to the fire.

"What did you get for one across?"

"The same as you: ASHES."

"It can't be a coincidence."

"Of course it can. Take a seat."

Ruzzo slumped into the chair. He rubbed his eyes and coughed. He'd stood watching the house burn until the fire department finally put the blaze out around six in the morning. Cavanaugh stayed by his side the whole time, getting back to Precious Acres at around eight.

Ruzzo showered and changed his clothes before coming to the station, but he still smelled like smoke. Or maybe it was Sgt. Badeaux.

"What did they find?"

"Not much. Most of the rubble will be too hot to touch for several days yet. Even then, there's very little evidence that can withstand that kind of heat."

"Except the teeth."

"I guess that's true."

Sgt. Badeaux brought his feet down and leaned across the desk.

"I know you are looking for answers, but we might not find any. It's possible that they just ran off again. They have a lot of history together."

"They wouldn't torch the house if that was the case. Something bad happened."

"Maybe they would, maybe they wouldn't. You just have to accept that we may never know one way or another."

"Are you giving up on Mr. Adamoli too?"

"I'm not giving up on anybody. I'm just doing my job."

"That's not how it sounds to me, which is a little troubling since I know that you used to coach Randy Liddell."

Sgt. Badeaux brought a hand up and slowly removed his sunglasses. His brown eyes were set close together under bushy, salt-and-pepper eyebrows. The sides of his nose were red and calloused from the constant rubbing of the wire frames. Dark, purple circles sunk deep into his face, as if he hadn't had a good night's sleep in years.

"You're not the only one with secret information, Ruzzo. I know that Rolf Kostbar offered you a lot of money to kill Randy."

"How...?"

"I'm not as bad a cop as you want to believe I

am. But, for what it's worth, I don't think you're a murderer. If I did you would already be behind bars."

"Don't underestimate me."

"Spare me the tough guy routine. I think Shayna Billups has you so hypnotized with that body of hers that you made some bad decisions. Ain't no shame in it. We've all been there."

"Leave her out of this."

"She's in it whether you like it or not."

"You done lecturing me?"

Sgt. Badeaux slid his glasses on and leaned back.

"Almost. You know, I get the sense that you were a pretty good cop. Maybe not a Boy Scout, but smart."

"Meaning what?"

"I think we can crack this case, but you need to stop the bullshit and trust me."

"You sure you want a security guard as a partner?"

"Things don't have to stay that way forever. I already told you that I spoke with your chief in New York. Play your cards right and I'll put in a good word. Cop to cop."

Something clicked in Ruzzo's mind during the long silence that followed. Maybe his badge really was more important to him than anything else.

"You've got a deal. Where do we start?"

"With the basics. We've got a string of murders

on our hands and somehow they all tie back to you and New York."

"I'm not so sure about the New York angle any more. Not if you take Billy Randolph into consideration."

"Randolph just stuck his nose where it didn't belong. He came out of his coma, by the way. I got word this morning."

"That's great news. Can I see him?"

"He's awake, but his jaw's wired shut. He's also got some memory loss. Whoever did that to him wasn't intending to leave any witnesses behind."

"Christ."

"It's going to be a long, slow recovery for old Billy. But at least he's alive. We still have a case to solve in the meantime."

"Okay. I'll need to think about it a little more. Something's not sitting right."

"Me too, but don't take too long. My guess? We've only got maybe two days before the Feds are all over this."

"I didn't know the Feds were involved."

"They weren't until I had them check out your theory about Geratti."

Ruzzo was honored that Sgt. Badeaux had taken him seriously.

"What did they come up with?"

"The mobster you dug up was Giancarlo Geratti. The man that was killed at Precious Acres was James Geratti. No relation."

"Well, that should at least keep the Feds off our back."

"You can't put that genie back in the bottle."

The bar was mostly empty when Ruzzo climbed up onto his usual stool. He had slept most of the afternoon away and was just getting back into the world of the living. His intention was to buy Cavanaugh a few drinks to thank him for the previous night, but the groundskeeper didn't answer when he knocked on his apartment door at Precious Acres. The Rusty Pelican seemed like the next best place to find him.

"Ladies and gentlemen! Introducing Tommy Ruzzo, dolphin hunter!"

"Very funny, Mikey. You haven't seen Cavanaugh around, have you?"

"As matter of fact, I have. He borrowed the keys to my boat. Said he had somebody special he wanted to take out there."

"Good for him. It must take a patient woman to put up with that sense of humor."

"You're telling me."

Mikey set a beer down beside a shot of whisky, and poured a second one for himself. He raised his glass in a toast.

"Here's to Jesse Lee Cavanaugh getting laid."

Ruzzo drank it down, slamming his shot glass on the bar upside down.

"No refill tonight?"

"I've got a lot to think about."

"Fair enough, but don't get too worked up about Shayna Billups. She's been nothing but bad news for as long as I've known her. She and Randy deserve each other, wherever the hell they are."

"Watch it, Mikey."

Ruzzo took his can of beer and wandered over to a table by the window. The sun had just gone down and the sky was fading from bright orange to dark blue. There was a storm blowing in on the horizon. He could see tiny bursts of lightning licking at the ocean in the distance. Cavanaugh was going to have one hell of a night on Mikey's boat.

Ruzzo sipped at the beer and thought about his conversation with Sgt. Badeaux. If Liddell knew that Rolf Kostbar had put out a contract on him, who else knew? Maybe Rolf Kostbar was more desperate than he originally seemed. And the reasons for wanting Randy Liddell dead were probably much more complicated as well.

Ruzzo ran all of these scenarios in his head again and again, each time coming up blank. He was deep in thought when two unfortunately familiar women sat down at the table with him. They smelled of cheap cigarettes and cheaper perfume.

"Hey, hot stuff. We were hoping that we'd run into you tonight. You in the mood to pick up where we left off?"

Ruzzo was about to tell them how he really felt about their threesome when a thought popped into his head. He gave the woman nearest to him a kiss on the cheek and thanked them both on his way out the door. His phone was in his hand and he was dialing Sgt. Badeaux as he jogged.

"Are you still in the office?"

"Sure am. This is where I do my best thinking."

"Meet me at the *Sentinel*."

"Why?"

"I think that Randy Liddell is the illegitimate son of Peter Kostbar. He's been blackmailing Rolf and Heidi Kostbar."

"What's this all about?"

"The threesome. I mean, the Kostbar triplets."

Ruzzo arrived first. The front door of the *Sentinel* office was locked and the lights were out. He went around to the side of the building and picked out a medium-sized stone to throw through the back window. Sgt. Badeaux arrived in the nick of time, shining his flashlight on the unfolding scene.

"What the hell are you doing?"

"We need to get inside right away."

"Hold your horses. I have a key."

They went around front and unlocked the door. Ruzzo barreled through the newsroom and headed straight for the safe near Randolph's desk. He yanked the top drawer open, pushing the contents aside until he found the sticky note taped down inside. The combination was right there in thick black ink.

The weighted dial felt good as it sailed smoothly between numbers. Ruzzo twisted the lever and the heavy door popped open just as Sgt. Badeaux wandered over.

"What exactly are we looking for?"

Ruzzo reached into the safe and produced a box of microcassettes. He immediately started rifling through them, reading the handwritten labels as he went.

"You said it yourself. Randolph put his nose where it didn't belong. I think he might have solved the case, and it almost got him killed."

"I guess we're going to be here for a while."

Sgt. Badeaux took the seat across the desk. Ruzzo found the label he was looking for and popped the tape into the recorder. He hit play in the middle of the phone interview and let it roll in the background, turning his attention back to the safe. It was comforting to hear Randolph doing what he loved the most, asking probing questions. Maggie, on the other hand, was in full defensive mode.

"What about the third triplet?"

"We've been over this a million times. It's common knowledge that they were born triplets—Rolf, Heidi and Peter. There are birth records from when they were born, school records from their childhood, corporate filings from when they took over the company, and a missing person's report from when Peter disappeared. All public information. No big conspiracy."

"Why has the family never shared details of the disappearance?"

"They have no obligation to air their dirty laundry for your entertainment."

"Don't try to pretend that Rolf and Heidi Kostbar are private people. Their sins are legendary."

Ruzzo reached inside the safe and pulled out a tattered folder. The seam ripped as he lifted it, spreading a thick stack of Randolph's private documents out across the floor. Both men dropped to their knees to clean up the mess. Sgt. Badeaux snapped up several bank statements, a couple of outdated contracts, a college diploma and the lease for the *Sentinel* offices. The tape rolled on.

"Oh, please. First of all, that was a long time ago. And second, it's not as if Peter Kostbar was an angel. We're still dealing with paternity suits twenty years later. But you already know all that because you write about this with alarming regularity. If you ask me, you're the problem."

"Speaking of which, has anybody interesting popped up recently?"

"Next question."

"I'm sorry. Let me rephrase that. Your latest paternity suit came to see me first, you know, in case you tried to make him disappear."

"Great. I assume you're talking about Randy Liddell. What a piece of work he is."

Both men looked up from the floor. This was what Ruzzo had been waiting for.

"Anything you would care to share about him?"

"Next question."

"There must be some validity to his claim if you aren't willing to deny it."

"I would be careful with this one if I were you."

"I guess I have my answer then."

"This interview is over."

They heard Maggie sigh as she ended the call. The recorder finally clicked to a stop when the tape ran out on Side A. Side B was totally blank.

"I think Randy Liddell actually was Peter Kostbar's son."

"Come on. I've know that boy forever. He

would have said something to me."

"How else do you explain the sudden windfall of cash? I think they got the results from the blood test and paid him off, or he was blackmailing them. Either way it would explain why Rolf wanted him dead."

"Because they would have to pay him off forever, or share control of the company with him. Goddamnit! I just wanted to believe he was dealing drugs again."

"The pieces definitely fit."

Neither of them spoke again while they considered how wrong they had been. For Ruzzo it meant that Maggie Walker had been in on the plot to kill Randy Liddell. Her last call was probably a plan the three corporate weasels in Tampa concocted to force Ruzzo's hand.

Well played, Maggie. I was just starting to like you.

It was Sgt. Badeaux who finally broke the silence.

"Something still doesn't make sense to me. Randy wouldn't go on a killing spree at Precious Acres after he started collecting all that Kostbar money."

"Maybe he was trying to create more leverage somehow."

"That would be insane. According to your theory, Precious Acres would be his cash cow. And what message could he possibly be sending by only killing New Yorkers?"

"Everybody except for Billy Randolph. Maybe Mr. Adamoli was right after all..."

Sgt. Badeaux jumped up and went over to the stack of papers he had collected off the floor. He shuffled through them until he came to Billy Randolph's diploma.

"I'll be. Looks like Randolph got his journalism degree from a New York university."

"What? I thought he was a local."

"Might as well be. He's been in Seatown for as long as I can remember."

Ruzzo stood up and started pacing. The pieces were all there, but he couldn't solve the puzzle.

"There has to be something obvious we're missing. Something about New York."

"Take it easy, Bubba. We might be barking up the wrong tree."

Ruzzo stopped in his tracks.

"What did you just say?"

"*Take it easy, Bubba?*"

Ruzzo threw the door open and started running for the harbor.

HAHA

All comedians love a captive audience, and Jesse Lee Cavanaugh was no exception. He was currently standing in the middle of the cabin on Mikey's boat doing a routine about New Yorkers. His material was killing.

"But seriously, folks. I've been to New York a bunch of times and I really love it, I really do. Except for the traffic, the noise and the crime. That's it. Oh, and the food, the buildings, the neighborhoods, the smell and all the stupid fucking people."

His punch line was met with utter silence, but Cavanaugh tried not to take it personally. The only other person on the boat was tied to a chair and gagged, after all.

"Tough crowd, tough crowd. Let's see. What else can I tell you about my time in the Big Apple?"

Mr. Adamoli's eyes were bulging as he fought to breathe. His face was red and tears were streaming down his sunken cheeks.

"Wait, here's a good one. So I was working as a road comic for a couple of years, you know, up and down the Eastern seaboard, when I finally got my big break. I was, I don't know, twenty-two years old. Anyway, a talent agent catches my act in Philly and offers me a gig at a famous dinner club in Manhattan. Naturally I jumped at the opportunity.

"So I went back home to Florida and got my act together. I worked on my material for a few weeks, bought a new suit and even rented a car for the trip. It wasn't cheap, I'll tell you that, but this was my big shot.

"Suddenly it's the night of the show. I arrive at the club in New York a couple of hours early and hang out in the dressing room backstage to get my bearings. In walks this beautiful cocktail waitress wearing a tiny dress. She was stacked, I mean *stacked*. This gal was way out of my league.

"She offers me a drink and we get to talking. Turns out she's from a little town not far from where I grew up. Just down the beach from here. I'm trying out a couple of my new jokes on her and she's laughing up a storm. Anyway, one thing leads to another and the next thing I know we're going at it right there on the dressing room floor. I still have rug burns, and this was like forty years ago!

"I'm thinking that this is already the best night of my life, right? And I haven't even gotten to the show yet. So we finish up and trade phone numbers, you know, pretend like we'll stay in touch. And then, just like that, it's ten minutes until show time. I put my suit back on, straighten out my tie and try to pat down my hair the best I can. That's back when I still had hair, of course.

"So the emcee introduces me and I walk out on stage. The room's dark and I've got lights in my face, but it doesn't take Superman's eyes to see that the place is filled to the rafters with thugs. They've all got these serious looks on their faces. You know the type: they make you earn the laughs. That's okay, I've worked in front of tough crowds before.

"But I don't get two minutes into my set when there's a big commotion in the back of the room. I try to soldier on, you know, be a pro for a few more jokes, but things start really getting out of hand. People are screaming, glasses are shattering. It's chaos.

"Next thing I know this giant gorilla is storming up to the stage and dragging the cocktail waitress from the dressing room behind him. Turns out she had a boyfriend. I know, right? So the place goes absolutely silent. I remember this because the microphone was feeding back something fierce as soon as he started smashing it into my face again and again and again. That got some of the biggest laughs all night.

"The last thing I heard him say was that I better not ever show my face in another comedy club for as long as I live. So here we are, on a boat, which, for the record, is not a comedy club. Just in case he's out there somewhere, you know, waiting to finish me off.

"Pretty funny, right? No? Well, there's a happy ending ladies and gentleman, because tonight I'll be doing all the laughing."

Ruzzo and Sgt. Badeaux were winded when they arrived at the harbor on foot. Mikey's boat was still in its slip. They could see Cavanaugh bouncing around the well-lit cabin. Back up units had been called in, but Sgt. Badeaux instructed them to standby in the parking lot. Nobody was exactly sure if they were about to catch a killer red handed, or interrupt a one-night stand.

"You sure about this, Ruzzo?"

"Sure enough to go over there and act dumb."

"And if he is the killer?"

"At that point I can stop acting."

"Great. What do you want me and the boys to do?"

"Stay out of sight for now. I'm sure you'll know when I need you."

Ruzzo started off down the dock. He was relieved to see that all of the nearby boats were dark. At least nobody else would get hurt if the shooting started. He could hear Cavanaugh talking loudly, as if he was giving some kind of speech. Ruzzo got within a few yards of the boat and called out, trying his best to imitate a drunken slur. He'd certainly had enough practice.

"Hey, Cavanaugh! You in there?"

Everything went still. Moments ticked by before Cavanaugh appeared up on the deck. The light from the cabin windows behind him made it impossible to read his face. His drawl was slow and steady as usual.

"That you, Ruzzo?"

"I heard you were having some kind of party tonight."

"I guess you could say that, but it's a private affair if you know what I mean."

"Oh shit! You have a date up there with you?"

"Something like that. What are you doing out here anyway?"

Ruzzo could see Cavanaugh craning his neck to survey the docks. He prayed Sgt. Badeaux and his men were still hiding.

"I got tired of The Rusty Pelican. Thought I'd come have a drink with you."

"You alone?"

Ruzzo spun around and made an exaggerated gesture with his hands.

"As far as I can tell."

"I guess you can come up for a drink or two. But don't get too comfortable."

Cavanaugh bent down and threw the rope ladder over the side. It hit the wooden planks with a slap.

Ruzzo climbed up and joined him on the deck.

"After you."

Ruzzo took a couple steps toward the cabin, but ducked before he reached the door on the port side. Cavanaugh was still standing in the same spot watching him when he stood up.

"Sorry. I tripped."

"Uh huh. You sure you need another drink?"

There was still no sign of anybody else. Ruzzo opened the cabin door and took a step inside. He caught a brief glimpse of Mr. Adamoli tied to a chair in the back corner of the room before Cavanaugh brought the pistol down across his head. It didn't knock him out, but he still fell to the floor in excruciating pain. Several swift kicks to his rib cage didn't help matters.

"You New Yorkers are always in such a hurry. I might have actually fallen for your little trick back there if you could just learn to...*Be. More. Patient.*"

Cavanaugh delivered three more kicks to underscore his point.

"I was just telling Mr. Adamoli the same thing, before you invited yourself over. But I guess that's okay because you're going to regret it soon enough."

Ruzzo looked up and noticed the red marks that were already turning to bruises all over the old man's face. His eyes were filled with absolute terror as they darted around the room. It seemed like he had no idea where he was.

"But where are my manners? I'm actually happy you're here."

"You could have fooled me."

It hurt to talk. It hurt to breath. It hurt.

"I did fool you, but mostly because Mr. Adamoli had you so worked up. He's been telling that crossword puzzle yarn to anybody who would listen for years."

"I thought you were my friend."

"I don't have any friends from New York. Now get up."

Ruzzo's ribs popped and cracked as he stood. Tomorrow was going to be rough, if he didn't die tonight. His odds weren't looking good given that Cavanaugh had the gun aimed at his chest.

"You must have nine lives."

"How's that?"

"I tried every way possible to pin these murders on you, but that idiot Badeaux just kept letting you slide."

"Sorry to disappoint you."

Cavanaugh didn't seem that surprised to hear Sgt. Badeaux's voice.

"Took you long enough to get up here, Bob. I saw the cabin lights reflecting off your glasses when Ruzzo came stumbling up."

"I was sitting out there hoping I was wrong about you, Jesse Lee."

"You were wrong about me, all right, for years and years."

"Meaning what? Are there more victims?"

Cavanaugh was inching forward as he spoke, his weapon still pointed at Ruzzo.

"Anybody ever tell you how stupid you look in that get up of yours, Bob?"

"Tell you what. Put the gun down and I'll dress however you'd like."

Cavanaugh stepped behind Ruzzo and leveled his gun at Sgt. Badeaux.

"No. You put your gun down. Don't make me shoot you."

"But I'm not from New York. Isn't that what this is all supposed to be about?"

"Fine. Have it your way."

Cavanaugh slipped his forearm around Ruzzo's neck and started pulling him back towards the cabin's starboard door.

"Tell your friends outside to drop their weapons and leave the boat."

Sgt. Badeaux took a small step forward.

"And if I don't?"

Cavanaugh swung the gun and pulled the trigger. The bullet tore through Mr. Adamoli's right shoulder, sending him backwards in his chair. He hit the ground with a groan. The pistol was back at

Ruzzo's temple before anybody had time to react.

"Do it."

"Everybody, this is Sgt. Badeaux! Drop your weapons and stand down!"

The order was initially met with a deafening silence. Ruzzo found himself reciting prayers he hadn't said in twenty years. And then, as if the heavens finally heard him, there was reluctant rustling all around the boat. Guns clattered to the deck and officers left the boat one by one.

"Yours too, Bob. No more negotiations."

Sgt. Badeaux set his gun down on the ground.

"This is the wrong choice."

"I didn't choose any of this."

Cavanaugh was breathing heavy as they stepped outside. The night air felt cold against Ruzzo's sweaty skin. They spun to face the rail and the groundskeeper relaxed his grip, shoving his hostage away. Ruzzo watched the cabin lights dancing on the water, wondering if this would be the last thing he ever saw.

There are worse places to die.

"Onto your knees."

Ruzzo turned to face him.

"Kill me standing up."

"You're always playing the tough guy. I'd tell you it was admirable, but it's just another New York cliché."

"What the hell happened to you up there?"

"It's a funny story. I wish I had time to tell you."

Cavanaugh brought his gun up and pointed it at Ruzzo's chest.

"It was a long time ago, Cavanaugh. Whatever it was."

"That's what you would think, but these monsters are always lurking in the shadows ready to pounce. I thought I had it under control after all these years, I really did. But then I got up on stage at The Rusty Pelican...Jesus, I bet Mikey's gonna regret talking me into that."

Ruzzo watched as a hidden officer emerged from the shadows near the bow. He took a few tentative steps toward them as Cavanaugh spoke, trying to get a clean shot. Ruzzo knew he had to keep talking if he was going to make it out of there alive.

"Killing me isn't going to change any of that."

"That may be true, but it's the only thing that makes me laugh these days."

The officer fired a shot that *pinged* when it hit the rail. Ruzzo pounced and tried to disarm Cavanaugh. They wrestled along the rail as Sgt. Badeaux charged. Cavanaugh's gun went off between them with a *pop* and Ruzzo collapsed.

The officer took a second shot that grazed Cavanaugh's leg. He stumbled back a few steps and smiled. Ruzzo halfheartedly lunged as Cavanaugh leapt overboard.

Ruzzo was draped over the railing now, his hand

on the hole in his gut. He watched the grounds-keeper plunge into the dark ocean waters below. The blackness swallowed both of them whole.

AWAKE

Ruzzo could just make out the soles of Cavanaugh's shoes in the distance. The water felt warm and thick, like he was swimming through gel. They had been underwater for a very long time when the ocean floor finally came into view. The groundskeeper seemed to land on the bottom when they arrived, as if he was jumping to the ground from some great height. He immediately started walking toward a lighted, coral cave with Ruzzo close behind.

Shayna was standing inside when they entered, tied to a stake. Her flowing blonde hair was dancing gently in the current. Little fish were flicking all around her naked body like a shroud of sparks. Ruzzo pushed past Cavanaugh and tried to reach for her, but his feet were sinking into the wet sand. He pulled on his legs with both hands and struggled mightily against the gravity that was sucking him down. She could only smile and wave as the flames rose up all around her.

"Shayna! Shayna!"

"He's awake."

Ruzzo struggled to open his eyes. A nurse put a

straw into his mouth and told him to take a drink. It felt like he was choking on the tepid water. She dabbed at his forehead with a wet sponge, the blurry memories bubbling up in his mind. There was no way for him to know how much time passed as he tried to break the surface.

Sgt. Badeaux was standing there when he finally did. He stepped forward and set the *Sentinel* crossword down on the bed next to Ruzzo.

"I'm not really in the mood."

"It'll be there when you need it."

"Where's Cavanaugh?"

"We have every officer between Miami and New Orleans looking for him. We'll catch him, if he's alive."

Ruzzo caught his own reflection in Sgt. Badeaux's mirrored sunglasses. He hated to see himself looking so much older.

"What about Mr. Adamoli?"

"His wounds are healing as good as can be expected, but—"

"What?"

Sgt. Badeaux gave the signal to clear the room. He didn't speak again until everybody else was gone.

"I wasn't going to say anything until you were fully recovered, but they diagnosed him with dementia. I guess it's pretty advanced."

Ruzzo could only blink in response.

"Come on. You didn't really believe all that crossword puzzle bullshit, did you? He was a high school drama teacher in New Jersey for forty years. The only thing he's guilty of is having a good imagination."

"But it can't be that simple."

"That's just how we like it in Florida, Ruzzo. Nice and simple. And before you ask, Shayna turned up at a women's shelter outside of town. Looks like she'd been there for a few days."

Ruzzo grimaced. Maybe Shayna didn't need him to save her after all. He was glad that she was safe either way. She knew where to find him, when she was ready.

Sgt. Badeaux was at the door when Ruzzo looked up again.

"Is Liddell dead?"

It was still hard for Ruzzo to say his name out loud. It was even harder for Sgt. Badeaux to hear it.

"We should know any day now, but I'm not holding my breath. Oh, before I forget. I brought you something. It's folded up in that newspaper."

"Thanks, Sarge."

"You can thank me by testifying against the Kostbars."

"I guess that means I should start looking for a new job."

"I heard Mikey was looking for a bouncer down at The Rusty Pelican."

Ruzzo reached for the newspaper as the door closed. A small bottle of bourbon slid from between the pages and onto the bed. He unscrewed the cap and took a swig.

The clue for one across caught his eye as he swallowed: "Word after wide."

Ruzzo woke up from his alcohol and narcotic haze sometime after midnight. The eerie hospital silence made it seem like the whole world was holding its breath. He could sense Shayna sitting on the bed beside him before he even opened his eyes.

"How long have you been here?"

The words escaped from between his teeth, but he didn't move his lips.

"A few hours."

She reached over and clicked the button on his pain medication pump twice.

"I've got a few things to tell you, Little Bear. It's best if you're comfortable when you hear what I have to say."

Ruzzo struggled to open his eyes, but the lashes felt stitched together. Tendrils of sleep were already climbing his legs and trying to pull him back down into the prickly numbness. Her voice sounded like it was coated in syrup as she told him the most incredible story.

"I'm sure you heard where I've been staying the last few days."

"Mm hm."

"It's a really nice place. The women there are very sweet. Stupid, but sweet..."

Ruzzo could picture the whole scene in his mind. A few of the residents at the shelter were standing on the porch waving. Shayna blew kisses as she watched them disappearing in her rearview mirror. Everybody agreed that it was a good idea for her to get out of the state and away from Randy Liddell. She was truly thankful for what those women had done. They were the best alibi that she could've ever hoped for.

Months of planning were finally paying off for Shayna.

"Of course I got pretty lucky too. I was originally going to use the money from the stolen cocaine to get some plastic surgery done. But our little party just kept going on and on. And then pretty soon we were broke. Honestly, Tommy, I have spent more time with you than almost anybody else since Randy."

Ruzzo conjured an image of Liddell that flickered between the handsome high school football star and a charred corpse.

Shayna heard through the grapevine that her ex-husband had come into money when she and Ruzzo were still in New York. She needed to find out for herself if it was true, but her most recent break up with Liddell had been the worst ever. So bad that she thought he would never take her back. She decided that her only chance was to make him jealous. And she knew nothing would get him more riled up than seeing her with a New York cop.

She took Ruzzo's hand in hers and gave it a little squeeze.

"He really was jealous of you, baby. I know it sounds like I used you, but it all worked out. You'll see."

It took a few weeks of living back in Seatown before she finally caught a glimpse of Liddell's shadow. Either his newfound wealth had turned him into a recluse, or he was finally turning into his mother.

"By then you were working at Precious Acres and we were living in that disgusting little apartment of yours. Do you remember that night at Brockton Beach?"

Ruzzo almost managed a little smile as she recounted the scene for him. The way she tore his clothes off and pulled him down to the sand. Ruzzo's sleepy smile faded as she explained how it was all for Liddell's benefit.

"I could practically feel his eyes on me the whole time. His first text message to me came when we were still in the golf cart on the way back to Precious Acres. God, he was so pissed off."

Ruzzo heard pride in Shayna's voice when she explained how she coaxed the big secret out of Liddell. It turned out he had no idea who his own father was until just before his mother died. And when she finally told him, he didn't have a clue what to do with the information. Mostly thanks to the fact that he had been half out of his head on pills for the last few years.

"And then one day he got the bright idea to get a paternity test done. That's when the blackmail started, right before I went back to live with him."

Getting Liddell to renew their wedding vows didn't take long, but she had to bide her time after that. Killing him and stealing his money meant a life on the run, and that wasn't what she was after. So what if she had to put up with a little physical abuse? It wasn't anything she wasn't used to. She just had to wait for exactly the right opportunity if she was going to make the most of this once in a lifetime opportunity.

And then the murders started a couple of months later and took up everybody's time and energy. Well, almost everybody.

"Sgt. Badeaux was the only person in town who seemed to suspect what I was up to. It almost put an end to my plans all together, until I thought of my white knight back at Precious Acres."

All she had to do was let it slip to Ruzzo that Randy was beating her. Even Sgt. Badeaux seemed to back off a little after her dramatic little performance at Sodee's.

"Seriously, Tommy. A wire? You are a terrible actor. Sweet, but terrible."

She gave his chest a little pat before she went on.

"Killing Randy wasn't hard, not after all the times he beat up on me. Maybe he really did blame me for ending his football career. Whatever it was, I got tired of it. This was the best solution for all three of us."

Ruzzo could hear his own heart monitor speeding up as she described the scene.

Liddell was nodding out on the sofa in the living room when she came in. The heavy brass lamp on the end table vibrated in her hand when she wacked him across the head with it. He was half conscious and staring up into her eyes as she strangled him. She almost got the sense that he was thankful she was doing it.

"That old house went up just like the biggest beach fire you ever saw. The only difficult part was maintaining my alibi at the women's shelter."

It turned out to be much easier than she imagined since it was an all-volunteer organization that was strapped for cash. The small staff there spent most of their time keeping the husbands and boyfriends out instead of keeping the women in. Shayna just told the other women that she needed some time alone to journal. With her bedroom door locked and some soft music playing on her stereo, she climbed out the window and headed for Brockton Beach.

"It won't be long now before Sgt. Badeaux's men find Randy in all those ashes. My guess is they'll try to pin it on Jesse Lee Cavanaugh. Then I just have to wait for that big old life insurance check to come in the mail."

Shayna giggled. Time would tell if she could lay claim to any of the Precious Acres fortune. It might be worth a little blackmail down the road at the very least, but that was just icing on the cake.

Ruzzo felt the mattress expanding like a cloud beneath him when Shayna stood up. He wanted to reach for her, but his arms felt like they were made of cement. The most he could manage was a whisper.

"Don't go."

"I have to, but we won't be apart for very long. If you can forgive me."

"Where?"

"I've always wanted to see Los Angeles. But don't worry—you'll know where to find me when the time comes."

Shayna gave him a kiss before she disappeared. Ruzzo nodded off and dreamt about California.

ACKNOWLEDGEMENTS

To my wife Heather and our beautiful kids, who give me the room to write. And to my beta readers and supportive friends, Scott Ross, Os Tyler, Paul Covington, Jeff Solomon, Erin Johnson and Travis Richardson. A special thanks to my talented editor Elaine Ash for being an early believer in this book, and my incredible lawyer, Kim Thigpen. And to Eric Campbell and the team at Down & Out Books—thanks for bringing *Crosswise* into the world.

S.W. Lauden is a writer and drummer living in Los Angeles. His short fiction has been published by *Shotgun Honey*, *Out of the Gutter*, *Criminal Element*, *Dark Corners*, *Dead Guns Magazine*, Akashic Books, *WeirdBook*, *Spelk Fiction* and *Crimespree Magazine*. His debut novel, BAD CITIZEN CORPORATION, was published in November 2015. The second Greg Salem novel, GRIZZLY SEASON, will be published in September 2016. CROSSWISE is his first standalone novella.

http://swlauden.com/

OTHER TITLES FROM DOWN AND OUT BOOKS

See www.DownAndOutBooks.com for complete list

By J.L. Abramo
Catching Water in a Net
Clutching at Straws
Counting to Infinity
Gravesend
Chasing Charlie Chan
Circling the Runway
Brooklyn Justice (*)

By Trey R. Barker
2,000 Miles to Open Road
Road Gig: A Novella
Exit Blood
Death is Not Forever
No Harder Prison (*)

By Richard Barre
The Innocents
Bearing Secrets
Christmas Stories
The Ghosts of Morning
Blackheart Highway
Burning Moon
Echo Bay
Lost

By Eric Beetner and
JB Kohl
Over Their Heads

By Eric Beetner and
Frank Scalise
The Backlist
The Shortlist (*)

By G.J. Brown
Falling (*)

By Rob Brunet
Stinking Rich

By Mark Coggins
No Hard Feelings

By Tom Crowley
Vipers Tail
Murder in the Slaughterhouse

By Frank De Blase
Pine Box for a Pin-Up
Busted Valentines and Other
Dark Delights
A Cougar's Kiss (*)

By Les Edgerton
The Genuine, Imitation, Plastic
Kidnapping

By A.C. Frieden
Tranquility Denied
The Serpent's Game
The Pyongyang Option (*)

By Jack Getze
Big Numbers
Big Money
Big Mojo
Big Shoes

(*)—Coming Soon

OTHER TITLES FROM DOWN AND OUT BOOKS

See www.DownAndOutBooks.com for complete list

By Richard Godwin
Wrong Crowd
Buffalo and Sour Mash (*)

By Jeffery Hess
Beachhead (*)

By Matt Hilton
No Going Back
Rules of Honor
The Lawless Kind
The Devil's Anvil (*)

By David Housewright
Finders Keepers
Full House

By Jerry Kennealy
Screen Test (*)

By S.W. Lauden
Crosswise (*)

By Terrence McCauley
The Devil Dogs of Belleau Wood

By Bill Moody
Czechmate
The Man in Red Square
Solo Hand
The Death of a Tenor Man
The Sound of the Trumpet
Bird Lives!

By Gary Phillips
The Perpetrators

Scoundrels (Editor)
Treacherous
3 the Hard Way

By Tom Pitts
Hustle (*)

By Robert J. Randisi
Upon My Soul
Souls of the Dead
Envy the Dead (*)

By Ryan Sayles
The Subtle Art of Brutality
Warpath
*Swansongs Always Begin as
Love Songs* (*)

By John Shepphird
The Shill
Kill the Shill
Beware the Shill (*)

By Ian Thurman
Grand Trunk and Shearer (*)

By Lono Waiwaiole
Wiley's Lament
Wiley's Shuffle
Wiley's Refrain
Dark Paradise

By Vincent Zandri
Moonlight Weeps

(*)—Coming Soon